FOURSQUARE BOOKS

Also by Nancy Parsons

More From The Better Mousetrap
with Dick Amsterdam

Bald As A Bean: The Experience of Sudden Hair Loss

Abigail's Unicorn

Ye Canna Join In Oor Games
Memories of a Scottish-American Childhood

Brothers of War: The P.O.W. Experience
with James F. Arsenault

The Dog That Managed Hedge Funds

TWO-THIRDS OF A GHOST

A Novel

Nancy Parsons

TWO-THIRDS OF A GHOST
Nancy Parsons

Published by
The Cheshire Press
52 Main Street
North Reading, MA 01864
www.cheshirepress.com

ISBN: 978-0-9853689-7-5
Library of Congress Control Number: 2013935050

Printed in the United States of America

This is a work of fiction. Any resemblance to individuals or occupations are
purely coincidental. All trademarks used herein are for identification
only and are used without intent to infringe on the
owner's trademarks or other property rights.

Parsons, Nancy
Two-Thirds Of A Ghost

For Dick

TWO-THIRDS OF A GHOST

"So, how do we go about this?" Lang asks casually, drink in hand, in an early scene.

"I interview you and turn your answers into prose," comes the sober reply.

And there, in a nutshell, is the art of ghostwriting.

Jonathan Campbell

Chapter 1

"Nobody but a fool ever wrote for anything but money."

Oh, who said that! Hemingway, Nell guessed, but finally—vexed—she looked it up. Ben Johnson! And all the way back in the seventeenth century too. Nell had to grin. As long ago as that, writers were hounding after the dough. Probably even earlier. The guy who came up with Beowulf was likely looking for a payoff from some wealthy Anglo-Saxon patron.

Well, whatever—the sentiment suited Nell right down to her socks. She'd been a writer for far longer than she admitted, and she was no fool. She liked to say she'd written everything except poetry and pornography, and she, Nell, definitely wrote for money! Let others pine to see their names in print; as long as her name was on the checks, she didn't need to see it on the book covers. Nell was a ghostwriter—a hired pen. Maybe that's not what you said anymore though. Then what? A hired keyboard? Didn't have the same ring. And with her last assignment completed six weeks ago, she was beginning to look forward to meeting a new potential client, to starting a new story.

She'd used the six fallow weeks to good advantage though. She'd cleaned the house from attic to cellar, made up three batches of soup for the freezer, and driven up to Damariscotta to spend a few days with an old friend.

When someone asked Nell how she acquired her clients and ghostwriting assignments, she was vague.

"They just show up," she'd say. Or, with a shrug, "It's a mystery to me."

But the leads came in—over the transom usually. Or somebody knew someone else who wanted to write a book but lacked either the time or talent to do the job. Or a former client passed her name along with some good reviews about her work. And often Robert Hutchins, her friend and sometime-agent, turned up a client from who-knew-where. Robert had connections all over Boston and into the wider circle of surrounding towns.

Nell lived in one of the surrounding towns. Well, she did if you considered Newburyport surrounding. Nell didn't think of it that way, but she had come to understand that Bostonians believed their territory—which they called greater Boston—extended as far as Albany. Beyond that, there existed a plain—vast and vague—known simply as The Midwest.

All Nell knew about this new candidate was his name: David Kernow. She supposed Robert would fill in some more details on their way to Lexington tomorrow when she would meet him. So actually she knew two things: the fellow's name and the town where he lived.

In the meantime, on what could be her last day of freedom from deadlines and the tyranny of computer and digital recorder, Nell was savoring the light of a brilliant morning. She had both elbows on the kitchen counter, her nose almost touching the rim of her coffee mug. So, with her face positioned to receive the steam from the coffee and the sunshine blasting through the windows over the sink, she was surveying the room with satisfaction. It was everything she'd ever wanted in a kitchen and indeed, it was more than a kitchen. It was her office, her sitting room, her haven.

It only lacked a bed and a bathroom, and Nell had to access those in other parts of the house. But the proper sitting room and dining room at the front of the little house were all but closed off and unused, while this space—kitchen and snug—was her sacred place. Post-Lloyd, she'd renovated it and branded it as her own.

Nell didn't often waste thought on her former husband, the late Lloyd Bane, but when she did, it was with a mix of irony and humor. If she'd just hung on for a while longer, if she'd stayed put inside that warped and crippled marriage instead of pushing through with the painful and terribly expensive divorce, then she'd be collecting the benefits now from Lloyd's significant life insurance policies, stock portfolio and 401(k), because three months after the divorce was final, Lloyd dropped dead on a treadmill in the gym. Nell read about it in the paper.

Was the trade-off worth it? Worth cutting herself off from all that lovely loot and spending a packet to break free of Lloyd Bane? She'd asked herself this a hundred times—perhaps just to experience, once again, her own answer. What was breathing worth? Oxygen? Life? Worth it? *Yes*, worth every cent and more.

Lloyd had loathed change—all change. And he had insisted that their antique cape on this Newburyport backstreet remain as a little museum to life in 1850. Or the way he imagined life in 1850 except with central heating and indoor plumbing. Nell had dearly longed to remodel the kitchen, but Lloyd was adamantly against it. She'd finally given up complaining about banging pipes, freezing floors in winter, and window panes that chattered whenever a nor'easter blew in across Plum Island.

Instead, Nell had struggled on, preparing their meals in a servants' kitchen from the last century—*early* in the last century—amid dark, varnished cupboards that reached the ceiling and in a murk that was tempered only slightly by the one small window.

So, post-Lloyd, she called those kitchen designers whose showroom was just off High Street, and directed them to tear down the wall that opened the kitchen to the snug, to push out the back wall a few feet and to install *windows!* Big ones. Marble counters, yes. Calcutta Gold, no less. She'd insisted on those and had shrugged off the warnings of stains. The microwave oven was cleverly fitted into the island. And as a finishing touch, Nell took a bonus check from a memoir commissioned by a well-satisfied yachtsman named Angus Titus and splashed out on an Aga Companion. Cream color. The perfect thing for making soup.

Nell believed deeply in soup. She believed in the therapeutic process of making it and in the therapeutic benefits of consuming it. She believed in the communion of sharing soup with someone you loved or with someone you scarcely knew. She believed in the good ingredients that went into soup, and she celebrated the stockpot, the immersion blender, the astonishing variety of recipes, and above all, the fragrance that simmering soup established inside a house. Soup was the perfect supper when you were home alone, especially after a long day listening to a client's story. It was easy to heat up and to sup, seated before the fire in the snug. A house became a home when there was a pot of soup on the stove. And if an apple happened to be baking in the oven, glazed with cider and dusted with cinnamon—well! Then she was assured she was home.

She frequently gave the Aga an affectionate pat on its cream enamel in passing and cast a fond thought into the ether toward Angus Titus. She glanced now at the Aga and thought of the quarts of soup thriftily prepared in the days of her leisure, now about to close. But Nell was philosophical. This new assignment would bring new experiences—new troubles, certainly, but also new rewards.

And, as ever, she was curious.

∽

Chapter 2

"So, how do you know this guy?"

Nell settled herself into the passenger seat of Robert's car. Even as she asked the question she was wondering how Robert kept the vehicle so pristine. The Mercedes's black hide never had a fingerprint nor a mote of dust. Nell had the ability to partition her mind, asking questions and absorbing the answers, even while she was collecting information about her surroundings—colors and facial expressions, scents and the words to tunes playing in backgrounds.

"I don't know him well, actually."

Robert steered into the flow of traffic on Route 95 and headed west toward Lexington. "I've met him twice—both times at fund raisers. He seems a friendly chap, and I've made a few inquiries about him. Quite personable. I think he'll be an easy subject—easy to talk to. Very forthcoming."

"Huh," Nell said, considering.

A slip of paper was sticking out of Robert's ashtray. A receipt for gas, she supposed. It reminded her of a glamorous fashion model with a single lock of hair askew. "Nothing in life should be perfect," Nell quoted to herself.

"So why does he want to write a book?"

"You'll have to ask him, of course, but he hinted at a life-changing experience. Something about 9/11."

"Huh."

Robert's GPS ordered them off the highway and sent them down a series of side streets that changed into curving roads. Just as Nell always connected Newburyport with the homes of prosperous merchants enriched by the sailing trades, she associated Lexington with the big Colonial homes of wealthy gentlemen farmers. Buckman Tavern sorts of places. She was surprised, therefore, to hear the GPS's nasal announcement, "Arriving at destination."

A contemporary house—seemingly all glass and great slabs of red wood—sprawled across the lot. She and Robert paced up the curving driveway, and a few seconds later, there was David Kernow opening the door. His eyes moved swiftly over the pair, pulling in first impressions. Nell noticed this even as she was doing the same thing. Kernow's face spread into a smile that was wide and welcoming.

"Come in, come in!"

And he stepped aside in a hostly manner. Handshakes were exchanged, and grips quietly assessed. Nell noted that Kernow's wide hand was warm and strong; his handshake, of course, was firm, just verging on painful. But Nell had long ago learned to give as good as she got, and she knew her own greeting equaled, Kernow's in forcefulness and confidence.

"Hutchins," their host nodded at Robert as he prepared to inflict his handshake, "good to see you again."

"And this, of course, is Nell—Eleanor Bane." Robert nodded toward Nell.

Nell was computing impressions rapidly. Kernow himself was powerfully built, not tall but still carrying hints of the varsity wrestler he had probably been; although he was extremely pleasant, there was still something pugnacious about him—perhaps it was the stance on the balls of his feet or the slight forward thrust of his upper body. Mid-fifties probably. Dark hair, quite thick and coarse and going a bit to gray. Business casual. Discriminating taste.

"Do you appreciate midcentury furniture?" Kernow asked. "I have quite a passion for it."

He swept his arm, pridefully indicating his interest. The living room, two steps down from the foyer, was enormous and arranged as if for a photo shoot with kidney-shaped tables, lamps in vivid, Fiesta-ware colors, a pair of stiff Knoll sofas and a chair that even Nell recognized as vintage Hans Wegner.

She cleared her throat carefully. Complete honesty between writer and client was essential.

"In truth, Mr. Kernow," she said drily, "I lived through the midcentury once. The style made me uncomfortable in 1958 and, *Birth of the Cool* notwithstanding, I haven't changed my mind since it's come back."

Kernow regarded her as if she were a pair of shoes he had contemplated buying until he turned them over and discovered the soles were cardboard.

To atone, Nell continued, "You have an enviable art collection though. I'm impressed."

Mollified, Kernow generously conducted a tour. Here a framed drawing by Alexander Calder, a Joan Miro etching there. A piece by David Paul Seymour hung between a Man Ray lithograph and a Jean-Michel Basquiat print that looked, to Nell, like graffiti.

"We'll go through to the study."

Now David Kernow extended an arm to direct the way to a room on the other side of the foyer.

It was a pleasant room. Landscaping grew close to the wall of glass behind Kernow's desk. A bit overgrown for Nell's taste; she would have gotten busy with hedge trimmers and clippers. A pair of chairs invited visitors to sit across from the desk, but there was also a table, designed perhaps for small conferences, at a right angle to the desk arrangement. It was here that David Kernow placed himself, indicating that Nell and Robert were to sit across from him. He folded his hands and placed them on the table as a signal that they were getting down to business. His heavy metal ring—Nell noticed the Brass Rat—claimed attention with a clank. He scrutinized Nell for several seconds.

"I assumed you'd be younger," he said.

Nell calmly held his gaze.

"Well, you know what they say about the word 'assume'... that it makes an ass out of you and me."

She smiled contentedly. She did not tell him his mouth was open.

Now she knew something about her soon-to-be client.

Kernow, perhaps in some vestige of embarrassment, cleared his throat.

"Tell me about the process of ghostwriting."

"I'll be delighted to do that, Mr. Kernow, but first I'd like to know why you want to write a book. And I'd also like to know what I'm to call you—*Mister* seems terribly stuffy, and if I'm going to essentially live in your socks during this process, I think we should be less formal."

He chuckled. "I couldn't agree more. And I'd like you to call me Deke. I was known by my initials when I was a kid—D.K.—and it quickly changed to Deke."

"It suits you," Nell told him. "Now about your reasons?"

"Well it's quite a story—do I call you Eleanor?"

"Nell is fine. Please go on."

"I'm a successful man, Nell. What they call an entrepreneur, although I've always thought that label sounded rigid. I've started three companies. Three. Grew them right out of the ground and up into prosperity. Then I sold them, one at a time—each at a whopping profit, I might add—and started up a new venture. The first was a semiconductor company, the second was an LED firm— do you know what that is, Nell? An LED?"

Nell did. "Light emitting diode. Please continue."

"Oh. Good. Okay, the last one was a dot-com. Now we're coming to the meat of the story. I was in New York on business associated with Compu-Savvy, the dot-com, in September 2001. In Manhattan. Staying with a friend on the east side. But I was there to keep a business appointment that just happened to be on the forty-first floor of one of the towers in the Trade Center."

Here David Kernow paused for emphasis. He looked meaningfully at Nell to see if she was appreciating the drama that he was foreshadowing. Since Nell remained impassive, it was impossible for him to tell if she was impressed with the gravity and horror of the tale he was about to tell.

~

Chapter 3

Nell, aware of Robert sitting in the chair next to her, was glad he was there. She planned to grill him later on his impressions of David—Deke—Kernow, especially about the man's reasons for wanting his tale transformed into a book. A touch of megalomania perhaps?

A carafe stood at Kernow's elbow. He poured himself a glass of water and drank it thirstily, as if the story that was just behind his eyes had parched him. By way of offering his visitors each a glass, he lifted the carafe and his eyebrows slightly. They both shook their heads to decline the offer.

"Well." With an effort, Kernow pulled himself back into the drama.

"My appointment was for 9:00. *Nine o'clock,*" he repeated, "only the damnedest thing happened. And at the time I was furious about it. Tear-ass! I was a few minutes behind schedule back at the hotel and I was grabbing papers, reports, all the stuff I'd prepared for the meeting and shoving it all into my briefcase. But I couldn't find a statistics report that I'd had made up just for the meeting. I mean, the whole point of the meeting was to focus on that report. My secretary had failed to put it in my briefcase. My

God! I phoned her. 'Where is it?' I screamed. And do you know what she said?"

Deke leaned across the table toward his visitors.

"Do you?" he demanded urgently. "Can you imagine this?" His voice shifted into falsetto. "'Oh, Mr. Kernow, here it is, right on your desk. Oh, Mr. Kernow, I'm so, so sorry. I'll fax it to the client's office right away.'"

Kernow seemed to release the persona of the hapless secretary.

"So now I'm digging around for the fax numbers for the office I'm supposed to be visiting, like *now*—the office in the Tower, you know. Finally I find it, I read it to the airhead, and by this time I know I'm going to be good and late. So I grab a taxi and tell the guy to step on it. Which he did. And he gets me down to the financial district just in time to see the first plane hit."

Deke stopped. Drained. He put his hand over his eyes for a moment.

"Well. There's more to the story, of course. The drama of it and what happened afterward and all. And I'll get into all that when we actually begin the writing work. But the point is this: that I escaped certain death by minutes. Seconds. And a terrible death! You can't believe what I was eye-witness to. I gave my secretary a handsome raise, by the way, when I got back to Boston. But for her carelessness, I'd have been sitting on the forty-first floor when the plane hit. So my life was saved for some reason and I had to wonder, saved for what? And although my life had been saved, I'd been through an event that was life-shattering but also life-changing. I was never going to be the same person again. And that's what I want my story to be about. That, and what I did out of gratitude and humility, for what came next was the foundation I established—The Children of Woe Fund."

He gave Nell a look that was penetrating.

"Now, Nell Bane, are you the writer who can tell my story?"

Nell had been silent for quite a while, and she had to clear her throat twice before she could properly speak.

"I am a ghostwriter, Deke," she said quietly. "And I'm a professional. I've written the stories of a number of people. Your story has more drama, I'll admit, than most I've encountered, but if you can tell your story to me, I can write it and bring to it passion and cohesion and a style that is strong and uniquely yours. I will learn your voice, and I will write in your voice."

Deke stared at her for several seconds. Then he nodded abruptly. "Good enough. I'm not sure why, but you sound plausible. Now tell me—how does this ghostwriting work?"

At last—her own turf. Here, Nell was very sure of herself.

"We'll establish a regular meeting schedule, Deke, say every two weeks for about two hours each a time. In those two hours, you'll tell me a story. You can start at whatever point you wish and stop when you want. You don't have to consider chronological order. I will take care of that in the writing. You can wander down any side-streets and byways you want as you tell your story. I call this yarnin'. Mark Twain was a great yarner."

Nell paused to assess how Kernow was processing this. When she saw no indication either way she continued.

"I will have my digital recorder running as you talk. I may ask you a few questions during a session, but usually not too many."

Nell pulled her slender Sony out of her bag and displayed it to Deke.

"Sorta small," he murmured.

"But mighty," Nell assured him.

"After our sessions, I'll return to my office and transcribe the recording. I'll use the transcription to write a first draft, which I will prepare for you to read."

"Why not just use the transcription word for word?" Deke wanted to know. "What are *you* getting in there for?"

"Because the written word is a good deal tighter than the spoken word," Nell explained. "I'll edit out the 'ums' and 'ahs'. I'll word-smith—that means straighten out tenses and syntax, use strong verbs that brighten your narration, and make certain that your details are consistent. That and a lot more. We don't want you sounding like an unlettered seventh-grader turning in a homework assignment."

Nell could see her would-be client was listening carefully.

"After I've listened to you in person, Deke, and have heard you tell the story again several times on the recording, I will not only know it well, but I will also have your voice inside my head. I will literally think like you for the duration of our work together."

"Will you require credits on this book?" Deke asked. "I mean this is supposed to be me and all. I'm supposed to be the author."

"Do you mean will the book cover say David Kernow's Story as told to Nell Bane? No. You're paying me to ghostwrite, Deke. No one need ever guess that it wasn't you at the keyboard."

Nell had a sixth sense about potential clients, and her sense now told her that Deke Kernow wasn't completely sold. He wanted to believe her, but there was an underlying suspiciousness that was still blocking his acceptance—a sort of "what's-in-it-for-you and how-will-you-screw-me? suspiciousness. However, he appeared to kick this aside suddenly and turned the conversation to business.

"So how do you charge for this ghostwriting? What's it going to cost me?

Nell named her figure. This was met with silence. Nell, her composure unruffled, waited. When Kernow shifted slightly in his chair, she smiled, but only inwardly. She knew she had him.

"Okay." He was gruff. "I suppose you'll want the money up front."

"A third when we start," Nell replied. "Then a third when I've finished all the interviewing, have collected all the information, and have written a first draft. This will be approximately at the two-thirds point of the project. I'll recognize when we're there and I'll invoice you. The final payment will be due when the manuscript is delivered."

Kernow examined this plan, could find no fault with it and finally nodded curtly.

"So now what?"

"Just one more thing, Deke. I am interested in why you want to do this book—in why you're willing to take the time and to spend this amount of money to publish your particular story. What result are you aiming for? What do you want to see happen when the book is published?"

"Ah." For the first time, Deke leaned back in his chair and relaxed. His face was transformed by a smile that Nell, in her writing mode, might have called radiant.

"What I want," he said, "is to see my story made into a movie. And I think it would make a brilliant movie. A thriller! I can see it: the smoke, the noise, the sirens, the chaos. I was there! I saw it all, I smelled it, hell, I *lived* it!"

"And who," asked Nell drily, "do you see playing the role of Deke Kernow?"

Deke actually looked surprised that Nell herself couldn't see. "Why Harrison Ford," he answered, "of course. I want you to write a thriller, Nell Bane. A thriller that Harrison Ford will give his eyeteeth to play. Now when can we begin?"

❧

Chapter 4

"You're very quiet," Robert said as he piloted the car back onto Route 95. "You haven't said two words since we left."

"Just processing," Nell admitted. "Listen, Robert, did you catch that reference he made to the hotel? I mean, he started off saying he was staying with a friend on East 89th street and then, when he talked about packing his briefcase, he said he was in a hotel. Did you notice that?"

"Frankly, no," Robert said. He thought for several moments. Nell had the impression he was recreating the conversation and trying to sort it through. "No, I have to say I don't recall it at all."

"Perhaps I'm mistaken," Nell said. But something had stirred her sense—not a scent exactly, but something. She shook her head as if to clear her mind.

Robert turned into the Burlington Mall parking lot and aimed for Crate & Barrel where Nell had parked her car when they had agreed to rendezvous at this halfway point and from there, car pool to Lexington for the meeting where Robert would make introductions. Robert pulled into the space next to Nell's Saab, but she continued to sit. Still thinking, apparently.

Robert prompted her. "So what are you going to do now?"

"I am going to drive home." Nell was decisive. "I am going to process the events of the day and make a decision about this client. And I am going to make soup."

Robert was familiar with Nell's soups. "What kind?" he asked now.

"Tuscan kale with white beans. And maybe some bacon."

"Yum-yum. Maybe I should have picked you up in Newburyport after all."

Nell smiled and patted his knee.

"I'll save you a bowl. Thanks for the introduction to David Kernow, Robert. We'll see how it works out. And thank you for driving."

"Let me know what you decide."

"I'll call you," Nell promised as she closed the Mercedes's door.

Robert slid the car into gear and rolled smoothly out of the parking lot, heading for Beacon Hill, and Nell, following, turned her tires onto 95 as well and stayed on it until the highway turned north and carried her all the way to Newburyport.

Nell had decided on Tuscan kale soup because it was fiddly and time-consuming and while she chopped and simmered ingredients, she knew the impressions of Deke Kernow would be simmering just below the surface of her consciousness. Methodically, she gathered the ingredients of the soup and began picking over the beans—Great Northern white beans—the first step of the soup-making.

TUSCAN KALE SOUP WITH WHITE BEANS

1 pound of Great Northern white beans
2 onions, coarsely chopped
1 garlic clove, finely chopped
2 quarts of good beef stock

2 quarts of water
A single 3-inch x - 1-inch rind of Parmigiano-Reggiano
2 teaspoons salt
1/2 teaspoon coarsely ground black pepper
1 bay leaf
1 teaspoon finely chopped fresh rosemary
1 pound smoked sausage such as kielbasa, sliced crosswise 1/2 inch thick
1/2 pound smoky bacon, cut in bits
8 carrots, cut in coins
1 pound kale, preferably Tuscan, with ribs removed and leaves coarsely chopped

In a pot, Nell covered the beans with one quart of cold water which she brought to a boil. Then she pulled the pot off the heat and let the beans rest in the water for an hour. She rinsed the beans and sautéd the onions until they were soft, then added garlic. Next, a quart of water, stock, beans, Parmigiano-Reggiano rind and seasonings went into the pot to cook until the beans grew soft. Meanwhile, Nell browned the sausage and bacon bits and after an hour or so, stirred the meat into the soup along with the carrots, kale, and remaining quart of water.

Nell took liberties with the recipe, throwing in whatever "extras" she found, which in the case of this soup was some orzo and some canned red kidney beans. That rind of cheese that had been knocking about the fridge for some time influenced Nell's decision to make kale soup. Once the first round of ingredients was suitably brought together and the soup was chuckling to itself, simmering away on the Aga, Nell triple-wound a scarf about her neck and took a brisk hike up to High Street where the warmth and fragrance of Fowle's Market descended like a pleasant cloud as soon as she pushed through the door. At the meat counter, she bought a pound of homemade linguica and a half-pound slab of bacon. She selected a wedge of Parmigiano-Reggiano to replace the supply she'd just used up, and she perused the stock for a while, taking her own inventory of comestibles that she might use in the future. She shared a few words with the young woman behind the meat counter, then a few more with the young man at the cash-out who sang out, "See ya later, Mrs. Bane" as she headed out the door and turned toward home.

The crisp air and exercise, combined with the restorative process of soup-making, cleared Nell's head and restored her good humor.

At home, she made two phone calls, one to Robert to announce her decision to accept the assignment as Deke Kernow's ghostwriter, and the second to Kernow himself to set the first appointment.

~

Chapter 5

Deke Kernow's greeting was warm as he swept her into the study. Like the rest of the house, this room was a homage to retro chic. Nell was ceremoniously seated at the table in a steam-bent stick chair. She took note of the teak sideboard and suffered a flashback that featured stacks of LPs and the syrupy drooling of Johnny Mathias. To reorient herself, she fished in her bag for the tools of her trade—notebook and pen and the Sony digital recorder. She checked for fresh batteries, and she was ready.

"Shall we start?"

"Well, I'm not exactly sure where to begin," Deke said hesitantly.

"In *Alice in Wonderland*," replied Nell, "the advice is to begin at the beginning, continue until you come to the end, then stop. That's not how this works though. You can start wherever you like. Storytellers weave their tales in bits and pieces. There is backfilling and there are detours and skips ahead into the future that at first seem unrelated and often confusing. Don't over-think context and chronology. Just let it all come out. I'll look at the bits and pieces later and knit them in a proper order. Right now, I don't know what that order will be—when the time is right, the stories themselves will tell me."

Deke looked slightly confused, and Nell took some pity on him.

"Actually, in this case, a good place to start is with the story you started telling last week when we met—the story of 9/11 and the way it changed the direction of your life. How would that be?"

"That sounds right," Deke agreed. Then he had another thought. "Oh, geez, no. *This* is the place to start."

The check on his desk was already made out to Eleanor Bane in precisely the amount she had mentioned—one-third of the estimated cost of the ghostwriting job. Deke carried it to the table and placed it before Nell.

"Thank you," she said. "It is always nice not to have to ask for the money. I appreciate it. And I also think it is a portent of an excellent client/writer relationship. And now, sir,...your story."

Across the table, Deke folded his hands and placed them, as though they were objects, on the table before him. His eyes became slightly unfocused; he seemed to be traveling back through memory to a more innocent time. A time when everyone was innocent together.

"I was still in the dot-com game at that point," he said. "I was getting a little stale though. I had grown the business about as far as I could—which was to the extent of my interest and besides, the dot-coms were going down left and right like dominos. So I was looking for a buyer. For someone or some outfit to take on the business and build it to a real, commercial success. And that's why I was in New York. I had an appointment to meet a guy whose office was in the Trade Towers. We'd been talking and were just about a handshake away from finalizing the deal."

"Name?" Nell asked quietly.

Deke looked up in surprise.

"I'm sorry. I try not to interrupt but the more specific you can be with details, the more authentic your story will be."

"Oh. Sure. Well, let me see. Cowan. Yes, that was it. Fred Cowan. Shall I go on?"

"Please."

"So I had this appointment to meet this guy Cowan on Tuesday morning, and I was going to take the Shuttle down early on Tuesday. But over the weekend, I changed my mind. I decided I'd drive down on Monday and stay with my old buddy from college."

He looked quickly at Nell and supplied the name before she could interrupt.

"John Altman. His name was John Altman. We'd been freshman roommates at MIT, and we'd stayed in close touch in the years since. Altman lived on the Upper East Side—on East 89th Street—he and his wife Kellie Winterspring."

Deke snorted with amusement.

"Winterspring! That was a hoot. That was not," he looked meaningfully at Nell, "her real name. She had aspirations as an actress. Unfortunately, her talent didn't match her aspirations."

He interrupted his own story to ask a question of Nell.

"So that thing you said about sidetrips and asides, I guess this bit about Kellie is one of 'em, huh?"

"Seems to be." Nell smiled. "Go on."

"So I got to Manhattan sometime Monday afternoon and finally found a place to park my car—my god! What is it about New York? Everything is inconvenient. Every damn thing you try to do takes three times longer than it should and is five times more expensive."

He shook his head.

"Well, anyway, I got there and we had a great time hashing up old times. We walked over to the York Grill for dinner, and when we got back, Altman and I and a bottle of Laphroig sat up till all hours talking some more. So the next morning—and I think I told you this—I was packing my briefcase to head over to the Trade Center when I discovered my damn secretary had let me come away without that report. I was sort of late to start with, and by the time she and I got the snafu straightened out on the phone, I was really late."

Kernow sat for a few moments in thought.

"So I tore down to the street, couldn't find a cab and had to jog down to Second Avenue before I finally found a free one and hailed it. I did notice, though—and this is really funny, because this impression has stayed so sharp and clear—I noticed, even as I was running, what a beautiful morning it was. What an absolutely glorious day! And then, when I was in the cab—and I told the cabbie to step on it hard—I leaned forward so I could look up through the cab window. The sky was amazing. It almost glowed that day; you know how sky glows just before the last morning star goes? The star burns brighter for a second just before the sky changes to dawn—then *poof!*—it twinks out. The sky that morning was so clear and blue it looked like I could drink it!"

Nell remembered. The sky over Manhattan that Tuesday must have been the same as the sky that had arched over Newburyport. Blue—the blue you'd choose if an artist's palette had been placed before you. And clear? Like spring tonic, it was so clear. It was a morning for drawing in enormous breaths of it. You couldn't get in enough of the air on that clear morning of September eleventh. And the incredible weather that morning was imprinted in her mind by the horror that had interrupted its serenity. Deke's description, however, was almost poetic. Nell was surprised and encouraged.

She waited. Deke seemed to be having some trouble pulling himself back to his narrative. He shook his head as if a mosquito was teasing his ear.

"Well. Where was I? Oh. So the cabbie is tearing down FDR, then he cuts over to—oh god, I don't remember how he went— but first thing you know, we were blocked in traffic. At a dead-mackerel stop. Finally we got moving again and he's getting us near the financial district and I'm thinking about how late I'm gonna be. And then it happened. And nothing else ever mattered after that."

Nell waited again. She waited for a long time and she restrained herself, almost forcibly, from prompting Kernow to continue.

"A fireball. And the sound. You could feel it as much as hear it. BOOM! The concussion was staggering. I mean the North Tower was within our sight. And *boom*. Time lost all relation, then. All meaning. I know the plane hit at 8:46. American Airlines Flight 11, but I didn't look at my watch or anything. Not then."

Deke's voice had dropped to a whisper, then picked up volume.

"'We're gettin' out of here!' the cabbie yelled. And probably if we'd done just that—right then—we could have made it out. Maybe he made it. I don't know, because I did what was probably a very stupid thing. I pushed the cab door open and jumped out. And I ran—yes, ran—*toward* the Tower. I can't think why. Instinct, I guess. I ran into a wall of people all jostling this way and that and then, it happened again. A second BOOM. This one we couldn't see because the view of the South Tower was blocked by buildings. The second plane hit. And that's when I knew something terrible—unspeakably terrible that had never happened before—was happening now."

Deke's voce grew husky.

"If an artist had to paint a picture of Hell, all he'd need was to be in Lower Manhattan that day. Stuff was raining down from the Towers, there was smoke, stench, people running, limping...and noise. Screams, sirens, fire—you could *hear* the sounds of burning. And then a new sound like the Earth was crumbling and the North Tower buckled at the knees and sank."

Deke Kernow stopped talking. Nell surreptitiously checked the Sony to be sure it was registering, for this telling could not be repeated. It was. She waited. Deke helped himself to water from the carafe. Finally he looked at her.

"I'm sorry," he said quietly.

"Why? What are you sorry for?"

But Deke only shook his head. He seemed unable to talk longer.

"Do you want to call it a day?" Nell asked gently. "We can pick this up another time. Later."

Kernow swallowed hard. He shook his head again.

"No. I can do this once, but I don't want to have to face it again. No retakes. Just give me a few minutes."

He pushed back from the table and, moving swiftly, left the room, closing the door quietly as he did so.

Nell continued to sit.

∽

Chapter 6

Nell checked her phone messages. She reviewed her email. She was about to launch a game of solitaire when the study door opened quietly and Deke returned.

"All right?" she asked.

"Sorry about that." He offered no further explanation. "Where were we?"

"At the Trade Center," Nell supplied. "Hell was in full throttle."

She leaned forward to turn on the Sony, clicking open a new file.

"Right."

Deke's hand came up to shield his eyes as he returned to that place and day.

"Okay. Sirens. Crap falling everywhere—paper, burning embers, and the *smoke*! My God! Emergency workers are running into that Hell and people are trying to run out of it. A young woman—she was crying—collided with me. Asian. No bigger than a minnow. She lurched sideways and started to collapse. I grabbed her and held her up. She was coughing. I'll never forget it. I never heard anyone cough like that before. She was just a little bit of a thing but these horrid coughs—raw, deep, almost inhuman—were coming up from her chest. She was gasping. I found out later her lungs were burned. Not just smoke inhalation, but *burns*.

Well, I held her up for a few minutes, but I realized we both had to get out of there, so I started trying to run—run north—and I'm half carrying her, half dragging her, and she's trying to tell me something.

'Don't talk,' I yelled to her, 'Don't try to talk!'

But she wouldn't shut up. She was trying to tell me about her kids—a boy and a girl. I had trouble making out what she was trying to say. Finally I slung her over my shoulder in a fireman's carry so we could make a little more headway. She wasn't talking by then but those hideous coughs would erupt every few seconds.

There were some EMTs near a corner and I left her with them. Never saw her again, but I knew her name. Rose Soon. Afterward—quite a while afterward—I managed to find out what happened to her. She died. Rose Soon died. I don't know how long after I left her; I don't know if she even made it to a hospital. And I don't even know what happened to those kids—that boy and girl who lost their mother on September eleventh."

Deke fell silent. Clearly, he was back in Lower Manhattan, and Nell didn't interrupt him. The Sony ran, recording the silence.

Deke returned to the present slowly. He seemed to emerge back into the space that was the study in the Lexington house with the midcentury furniture and collection of art.

"I was changed," he said simply. "We all were, I know. We lost our innocence that day, and we were never going to be the same again.

I went back to John Altman's. I don't know how I got there. I was too numb to notice. I do remember though, how solicitous John and Kellie were when I finally turned up. Their TV had been on all day, of course, and they'd never left the screen. They knew I was down there in the thick of it—knew my appointment was in the North Tower—and they had simply assumed I'd been on the forty-second floor when the plane hit and that there was no hope.

Well, they put me to bed in the guestroom and I slept for eleven hours straight. When I woke up it was Wednesday, the second day of horror. People were still trying to come to terms with what had happened—and of course, there wasn't really any way to come to terms with it. It was senseless. Almost everyone in New York had been personally touched by the horror. If they hadn't lost someone close, they were connected in some ways to people who had.

In the Altmans' building, the woman across the hall had lost her sister. Some guy two floors above was gone and he'd had a young wife and a six-month old baby. And then there were those two kids whose mother had practically died in my arms.

I was changed. I lay there in bed that morning—and I had a bed to lie in! I thought about my luck—a secretary's mistake, a report that hadn't been correctly packed, the trouble hailing a cab, the traffic snarl—all things that had intervened to trip me up. And ultimately save my life. But why had my life been spared? Why? Was I intended for some higher purpose? I determined right there and then that my life would take a different course. That I would do something for the families of those people who hadn't been spared. Something for that six-month old baby and for the children of Rose Soon.

I drove home to Boston that afternoon. Since I had my car, I could slip out of Manhattan. There was absolutely no public transportation to be had. Planes were grounded for a week. Trains were idle. And not just in New York. Everywhere. There wasn't a train or a taxi to be had. The city, after that terrible chaos was still. Silent. Eerily silent. I got my car out of hock as soon as I could, picked a circuitous route out of the city and finally got on the road to Boston.

On the drive, the Children of Woe Fund was conceived."

He slapped both palms flat on the table—either to punctuate

his narration or end it—and he looked a Nell fully for the first time since they'd begun the interview.

Nell consulted her watch.

"Whew!" she said. "That was a long session. Slightly more than two hours, but in emotional terms, miles. But I think we started with the most difficult material, didn't we?"

Deke nodded.

"Yes," she continued, "perhaps the rest of the story won't be so emotionally exhausting."

When he was silent, Nell waited a few moments, then continued.

"This is what I'm going to do: I will transcribe the recordings," she nodded toward the Sony, "and then I'll use the transcriptions, as well as the impressions gained from listening to your voice, to write a first draft which I will email to you in about a week. You read it and see what you think of it, and we will discuss it at our next meeting. Do you have a subject for that next meeting? Perhaps the story of how you established the Foundation?"

"Yes," Deke said. "Exactly. It will be easier from here. All downhill. Thanks for bearing with me, Nell. This wasn't easy to remember or speak about and I doubt that it was easy to hear."

Nell stood, put the cap back on her pen and packed her notebook and recorder into her bag.

"Wish me luck," she said crisply. "I'm going back into Lower Manhattan."

~

Chapter 7

For the third time—straight through, without stopping—Nell listened to Deke's account of being in Manhattan on 9/11. She pressed the "stop" button with her thumb and sat for a while in the silence, feeling depressed. She was following her customary ghostwriting practice of listening to her recordings until she had completely absorbed the subject's voice, verbal mannerisms, cadences, tonalities and probably some other things that she couldn't name. When Nell could begin thinking in her client's voice, she could at last be confident of her storytelling. Then she would transcribe each interview, going through the recordings once again, but now she forced herself to work at a pace that could, depending on diction and topic, be painstaking tedious. Deke's story bore an unusual load of heavy freight. Nell had not been in New York on 9/11, but like almost every other citizen, the day was seared into her memory. Impressions, sensitized by horror, had been imprinted indelibly. She remembered some elements of that Tuesday better than she remembered any of her own birthdays or even her wedding day or the day she and Lloyd had signed the purchase-and-sale agreement for the Newburyport house.

She sat now in the middle of the sofa in the snug, staring at the cold ashes under the grate in the fireplace.

"I should shovel those out, I suppose," she told herself. But she didn't move.

The sky above Newburyport that Tuesday would have been the same sky that arched over New York. The humidity had blown out, Nell remembered, leaving air so dry and crisp that you just wanted to bottle it and drink it. Except the sky above Newburyport had stayed blue all day, while the sky over Manhattan—at least the lower end of it—would have turned gray-black with a toxic, debris-filled smoke. It would be days before anyone would see a blue sky there again.

She'd turned on the TV that morning, not something she usually did, and had actually been holding a mug of coffee to her lips when American Airlines Flight 11 smacked into the North Tower. *The Today Show* hosts, Katie Couric and Matt Lauer, had seemed confused, but then, as information dripped in, they became slightly hysterical. Peter Jennings, apparently summoned from his home, took over shortly and his calm, measured reporting reassured Nell to a degree.

Soon, Nell would need to start the transcription, but she couldn't seem to bring herself to it. Instead, she called Robert.

His query—"How's it going?"—elicited such a limp response, that Robert promptly asked another question.

"How about coming into town for lunch? Walk up and down Charles Street. Look in some of the shops?"

Nell knew instantly that was the exact thing to do.

It was well past noon by the time she parked her car in the Common Garage, crossed Beacon and climbed Robert's steep street. The house he shared with Jerry Gasso stood smack against the sidewalk. She stepped up and into the perfect and precise space created by a designer (Jerry) for himself and a bibliophile (Robert).

Robert had a mild complaint.

"I came home to find Jerry had re-organized all my books."

Robert's gaze swept the bookcases that lined the sitting room. Nell's eyes followed his.

"He arranged them by *color*. By *blocks* of color. He thought the higgledy-piggledy look of too many different colors next to each other was jarring. Fragmented, he said."

Although Robert looked nettled, Nell could see amusement shimmering just beneath his expression of pseudo-frustration.

"I used to have all the philosophy books together, and there was a section for modern fiction and so forth. Now, if I want to read Kant, I have to remember that he is red. Schopenhaur," Robert continued with irony, "is orange. They no longer live anywhere near each other. Chaucer, for one, has come between them. As has *The Sound and The Fury*."

Nell smiled.

"Well," Robert shrugged, smiling also, "it is what it is. I thought we'd walk down to Beacon Hill Bistro."

"Perfect."

Over lunch—seared Atlantic salmon for Robert and duck confit with butternut squash risotto for Nell—she gave him a précis of Deke's 9/11 tale, finishing up with her own sense of frustration and depression as she delved once more into the ruins of the Trade Towers and the sorrow of the lives lost there.

Robert was sympathetic.

"It sounds like the worst of the emotion has been dealt with though," he said sensibly. "From here on out, the story should move upward into more positive directions."

Nell, sipping her coffee, had to agree and, warmed with a delicious lunch and the atmosphere of the Bistro, decided she was ready to get on with the work.

"There's one more piece of therapy for today," she said.

"What is that?"

"A stop into Linens on the Hill. It soothes my troubled soul to finger the high thread counts of splendid sheets and towels."

"Deal," said Robert, sliding his credit card back into his wallet. "Let's do it."

~

Chapter 8

Draft 1, Nell wrote. Then, with a deep breath—the sort of breath you draw as you pull every fiber of your body together in order to dive into an icy lake—Nell placed her fingers on the keyboard and began to write. She wanted to give Deke three samples so she could gauge his response to her narration and so they'd know whether he judged her emotional translation to be to his liking.

# # #

I suspected, from the first waking breath, that it would be one of those days. After the travel alarm misfired and I'd nicked my lip shaving, and after I found I hadn't packed clean socks, my suspicions were confirmed. The only bright thing that morning was the September sky outside the apartment window. It was spectacular—a color my wife calls azure. The apartment wasn't mine. I was staying with my old friend John Altman and his wife Kellie up on Manhattan's East Side. I had scheduled a business meeting on Tuesday morning at 9:00 down in the Trade Center, and at the last minute had decided to crash with the Altmans rather than bunk in some hotel room. So I drove down to Manhattan from Boston on Monday afternoon.

Then, when I heard Kellie Altman calling that breakfast was ready and how did I like my eggs? I made another unpleasant discovery. My secretary hadn't packed the papers that were critical to the meeting. Critical understated it. She'd left out the packet of financials we were going to discuss. Those figures were the whole reason I was even in New York. By now the travel alarm was pointing to 8:15, and my cut lip had just dripped a line of red dots on my last fresh shirt.

"Forget the eggs, Kell," I yelled as I made for the phone. I knew Janine wouldn't be in the office yet. When I'm out, she's always late, but I had her cell number and I punched it in hoping she'd kept the thing charged. Odds were 5-to-1 she hadn't. But she had! And when she answered, I let out a sigh so loud that Kellie turned from the stove where she was scrambling eggs for John.

After I'd yelled at Janine for a while and after she'd apologized about eight times, I asked her what the hell she was going to do about this, and to give her credit, she said she'd fax the financials directly to the office where we were having the meeting.

Great. So then we both went digging around for the fax number of that office—she on her end of the phone and I on mine—and meanwhile all kinds of time is being chewed up by the search.

"Listen, Janine," I finally yelled. "Keep looking for the number. Find it! Fax the financials! I'm outa here."

I yelled a fast good-bye to Kellie and John, grabbed my briefcase and was out on East 89th Street in under a minute.

Now is there ever a cab around when you need it most? I looked up and down the street and no sign of one, so I started sprinting up toward Second Avenue, and finally spotted one that slowed down. I didn't even give the driver long enough to fully stop. I simply hopped in and said, "Trade Center. North Tower. And for God's sake, step on it!"

The guy was good. He didn't ask any questions and his foot went down on the accelerator like he was stomping on a rat. We were off like a shot. And that lasted about a block.

I was leaning forward in my seat, as if that would make the cab go faster, but we just inched from gridlock to gridlock. Finally I could see the North Tower through the windshield. We were within striking distance.

And then it happened.

I saw the plane drive right into the tower, about two-thirds of the way up, it seemed to me. There was noise—percussion, really— that I could feel as much as see. I remember yelling something to the driver and he yelled too. I was leaning all the way forward and digging my fingers into his shoulder.

"We're outa here," the guy yelled.

"No!" I yelled back, "Go on!"

But he started to turn the cab around. I pushed the back door open and jumped for the curb. I remember hearing a tremendous screech of brakes as the cabbie jerked through a three-point turn and peeled out. And I—and I have no explanation why—started sprinting toward the confusion ahead.

"Are you crazy..."

#

She staggered out of the smoke, just a slip of a thing, and she lurched into me. Almost knocked me off base with the impact. And she was coughing—well, it wasn't like any coughing I'd ever heard. This was a racking sound coming from deep inside. I caught her in my arms and held her. Embers were falling all around us. Embers! Some were the size of chunks of burning coal. I held her and she continued to cough. I slipped my arm around her back and under her arms and we started to move away from the inferno, both of us staggering.

She kept trying to talk.

"No, no," I said repeatedly, "save your breath. Save your energy."

But she insisted. She wouldn't shut up.

"Soon," she was gasping. "Soon."

"Yes, yes, we'll be there soon. I'll find help—it won't be much longer. We'll get help soon."

But every time I said this, she grew more agitated, and she'd shake her head—all this long black hair was wild. "Soon!" she'd insist.

Finally I got it! That was her name.

"Soon is your name!" I told her.

She looked exhausted.

"Yes," she said. And then the dreadful, wracking coughing stated again.

"Rose," she wheezed, "Rose Soon."

I was mostly carrying her by now, but she still wouldn't shut up. She kept trying to tell me about her children—a little boy and a girl. If she ever said their names, I didn't understand.

"Save your breath," I kept saying. "Don't try to talk."

We must have staggered along for three or four blocks, and then I saw a first aid station or some kind of emergency triage outpost that some first responders must have set up, and I dragged Rose Soon over to it.

"Her name is Rose Soon," I told them. "She must have inhaled a lot of smoke."

She just slumped down.

"She didn't just inhale smoke," one of the EMTs said, "her lungs are *burned*." And he shook his head.

The last time I saw Rose Soon she was lying on a stretcher right down on the sidewalk and the EMTs were grabbing for a new victim.

"It's okay!" one of them yelled to me. "We'll take over from here. If you're smart, buddy, you'll get the hell outa here."

And I guess I did. Maybe I didn't. I don't know what I did. Can't remember. Maybe I tried to help some other people. I don't know. At some point in this drama the South Tower was hit. There was more shouting, more screams, another concussion, another explosion. Then North Tower was collapsing. Just crumbling. For some reason I thought of an old lady going down on a sidewalk because her pins had given way beneath her and she was just taken down gradually, gracefully, almost like it was something she'd intended to do.

But then, my god! The stuff that rose into the air! The smoke, the dust, the...I don't even know what all was in that cloud of destruction. And I was coughing too, like Rose Soon. I'd inhaled I didn't know what but my lungs weren't burned. Yet, I thought. And I was just driven back by the overwhelming finality of that holocaust...

# # #

East 89th Street was almost in darkness when I staggered to the Altmans' door. I remember that, but I don't know what time it was—maybe it wasn't even dusk. Maybe the sky was darkening with ash from the horror on the lower tip of the island. I don't know how I got to 89th Street—honestly, I don't. Nothing was running. No subways or buses. I couldn't have caught a taxi, so I must have walked all that way. I was limping, I know that. Blisters the size of half dollars had been raised on my heels. Those smart business shoes weren't made for long distance walking, that's for sure. My suit was filthy, a sleeve was torn, my tie had disappeared, how or where I had no idea. But I staggered into the lobby and leaned on John Altman's bell.

Then they were there, John and Kellie, and they were pulling me inside. Exclaiming. Shocked. They'd been watching TV all day and, knowing where I was, had me dead in their minds and were deep in mourning. I guess, to them, I must be looked like Lazarus raised from the dead.

I don't know. I just remember their voices and their loving concern. They helped me out of my clothes. John guided me into the shower, and I kept telling him I didn't want a shower. I just wanted to lie down and sleep. But the shower helped. It washed away the filth and the ash and some of the horror. I stood under that shower for who-knows-how long with my face turned up to the spray and the scalding water raining on my eyelids and cheeks like needles.

Kellie made a cup of tea, I remember that, and she kept encouraging me to drink it, but John had brandy. Oh God, I was grateful for that brandy. It burned like hell in my throat, and for some reason, that seemed justified. I should be burned. I had survived. Hundreds of others hadn't. Rose Soon hadn't. And somewhere in New York, a little boy and girl would be growing up without their mother.

But then I wanted to blot that out, those thoughts. I, who had cheated death, who had—for some unknown reason, been spared—I wanted to hide in sleep. I wasn't ready, then, to read any meaning into this, I just wanted to sleep...

~

Chapter 9

"Well, I read it."

Deke Kernow had placed his fingers in a here's-the-church-and-here's-the-steeple position—at least that's how Nell had always thought of it—and was tapping the steeple against his lips to indicate thoughtfulness. Nell waited. The first one to speak, loses she thought.

The silence lengthened.

Nell raised a single eyebrow. Did that count as losing? Maybe it was a winning tactic. It wasn't speaking anyhow.

"It's quite an experience," Deke finally said, "meeting yourself on paper like this. I've never experienced this before. It's something like catching the reflection of yourself in a store window as you're walking along a street and for a second you think, "Who the hell is that?""

Nell waited some more.

"Actually, I liked it," he finally declared. "The first time I read it, I confess I was distracted by the narrator—in other words, me! I thought, is that how I sound? Can't be. But then I read it again and, by god, I was pulled into the story. It was like I was there at the Trade Center all over again. My heart started to pound. I started breathing harder like I was running and poor Rose Soon was hanging off my shoulder. And when I was done reading, I just sat there feeling terrible."

For the first time, Nell smiled. She'd done her job well.

"That's what I'd hoped you feel," she said quietly. "Okay, Mr. Kernow, we've got the voice, we've got the momentum going, let's get on with the book."

Out came the Sony Recorder. Nell positioned it on the conference table and uncapped her pen.

"Are you ready to pick up with the trip out of Manhattan? You were going back to Boston and you told me that's when you changed. That's when the foundation was conceived."

Deke emitted a lengthy exhale.

"Right. That's where we left off."

He frowned. "I hardly remember the drive back—the Merritt Parkway, Connecticut rushing past by the car windows all the way up 84, then finally hooking up with the Mass Pike at Sturbridge and rolling east toward 95 ... I must have done that but I can't tell you a thing about the traffic. Whether it was light or heavy. All I could see were the faces of those two kids—Rose Soon's kids. My god, I didn't even know what they looked like. Had never met them. Had never seen a photo. But I swear to you, Nell, there they were. I could see their little faces, side by side peering through the windshield at me, grief in their eyes. Not crying, just looking—looking stricken."

The Sony rolled.

"By the time I reached Sturbridge, I knew what I had to do."

"Which was?" Nell rarely spoken during sessions, but Deke seemed stuck.

He looked toward her now. He seemed surprised to see her.

"I decided to establish a foundation, or a fund, to help Rose Soon's kids and all the other kids who'd lost parents in this—this horror show—this outrage we eventually started calling 9/11!"

Nell gazed at him encouragingly, waiting for details.

"So how do you go about setting up a charitable fund?" she asked.

"Setting up a nonprofit organization is relatively easy. Not rocket science. Even little neighborhood groups working at kitchen tables manage to establish nonprofits. But detail has never interested me, so I got in touch with an expert—a fellow I'd used off and on for several business deals. Fellow named Ira Zayder, an attorney, and he did all the legwork and red tape stuff. He knows all about nonprofits and the associated tax issues. He set it up and he continues to handle much of the business end of the operation. We also have a woman in charge of the office—bookkeeping, correspondence, telephones, all that sort of thing. *And*, we have a headquarters."

Here Kernow's smile turned ironic.

"Where?"

"Gloucester. On Rocky Neck actually. I found a renovated warehouse—an old sail loft or something. Got it for cheap money and renovated it further. The harbor side of the place is all glass. There's something about the sight of the water that's—tranquil, I guess. Yes, that's it—tranquil. It's a good thing for the charity to be set in a tranquil setting. It's like a promise."

"And what is *your* role in the foundation, Deke?" Nell asked quietly. "What part do you play?"

"I bring in the dough. That's practically a full time job. I raise two things: awareness and money. I organize fund-raisers and cousin-up to the big money sources. I probably know everybody worth knowing in Boston and New York and all around the conference tables in the really big boardrooms. I have connections and resources on every board in the northeast that could cough up big dollars."

"Would I have heard of this fund?"

"Almost certainly. I called it The Children of Woe Fund—a

charity for the Children of Victims of 9/11."

"Children of Woe," Nell repeated. "Sort of like Wednesday's child from the nursery rhyme? 'Wednesday's child is full of woe.'"

"Yeah. I wanted to use Wednesday's Child actually, but every third adoption agency in the country had claimed it."

"Well, The Children of Woe Fund has a certain ring to it," Nell said encouragingly.

Deke opened a manila folder, withdrew a sheet of letterhead and slid it across the table to Nell.

The sheet was professionally and tastefully designed, its four colors softened and muted soothingly, the type greyed, and the logo merely a few simple lines symbolizing something Nell couldn't identify.

Reading, Nell learned that the fund's mission was to raise awareness of the emotional and economic issues endured by the children of 9/11 victims and ultimately by all children worldwide who have been secondary victims of acts of terrorism. She scanned the document: a 501(c)(3) nonprofit organization that depended on the support of individuals, foundations, corporations and institutions to carry out its mission and that all donations enabling the continuation of the foundation's work were welcomed and appreciated. In recognition of this, commemorative wristbands would be given, and donors were to state the color of their choice— red, yellow or blue.

Nell raised her eyes.

"May I keep this?"

With a single, magnanimous gesture, Deke granted her request.

Nell sat back in her chair.

"I know very little about establishing a nonprofit," she admitted, probing. "Don't you have to come up with seed money or something?"

"Some, yes." Kernow was modest. He cleared his throat,

embarrassed perhaps to admit this. "I'm not without some means. Some inherited family money, and as I once said, the businesses I started up, I sold at rather impressive profits."

"Your business interests, and even your family background, are areas that I'd like you to touch on more deeply, Deke, but at another time. Tell me, though, has The Children of Woe Fund been successful?"

"Bottom line is this: we've raised just north of fifty million and have distributed almost ninety percent to children of 9/11 victims. That includes the children of firefighters and cops as well as the people caught in the Towers."

Deke fixed Nell with a penetrating stare.

"Do you realize," he said, "that there were 1,452 dependents of the people killed or injured in the 9/11 attack?"

Nell had not been aware of that figure.

Gratified by her expression of ignorance, he continued.

"Here's another statistic: approximately two-thirds of all American households donated some amount of money to charities associated with 9/11."

Deke suddenly came out of his chair. "Here! Let me show you something!"

And Nell found herself taking a photo tour. She was pressed along from frame to frame, each prominently featuring her client. There were presentations where Deke was offering checks and other presentations where he was receiving plaques of recognition. There was Deke behind microphones at press conferences and Deke standing belly-to-belly with celebrities and Fortune 500 notables, most holding cocktails. In one picture Deke was laughing and in another he was tenderly holding a child who looked to be about three, and it was obvious that he was holding back tears.

"Her father died just two weeks before she was born," he said quietly.

This photo seemed to depress him, and he returned to his

seat at the table. Nell quietly followed his lead.

"So the fund is your job now," she said. "You've not been tempted to start up another company?"

"No." He shook his head. "Since that day when my life was changed, nothing else has made sense. Everything but helping those children has seemed hollow."

"However," Nell pursued, "you'd admit that the money of the marketplace is what enables the fund to function and provide the fuel to sustain the mission?"

Deke shrugged. "That's true. But for me, money has ceased to be an end—a goal. It is simply a means to the greater good."

Nell consulted her watch.

"Once again, we've gone overtime," she said. "And once again the emotion and the subject seemed to require it. So I will transcribe this material as I did before and will email it to you for comment and correction if necessary. Shall we set another time to meet? And perhaps, now that we've covered the important material of the life-changing event and your reinvention of yourself, we could go back in time so I could understand more about the man you are. How you were shaped and raised, and how you became an entrepreneur."

"Sounds like a plan," Deke acknowledged. "A good one. I'll look forward to it. And I'll be eager to read the next installation of the life of Deke Kernow."

~

Chapter 10

Nell lined up the ingredients on the counter and reviewed them with satisfaction. For sheer vitamin quality, it was hard to improve on souped-up split-pea soup. Besides, while the soup simmered on the Aga, she could return to Deke Kernow's story.

Nell enjoyed the mindless chores of peeling and chopping vegetables. With her hands occupied, another part of her mind was free to review the details Deke had provided of the founding of the Children of Woe Fund. It occurred to Nell that hundreds of such funds must have been established after 9/11. She dried her hands on a paper towel, set the lid slightly askew on the stockpot, and carried her laptop to the island.

On Google, she searched on 9/11 charities. Although she had reasoned there would be a number of funds with similar missions, she wasn't prepared for the staggering number of nonprofits dedicated to helping the families of 9/11 victims. How, she wondered, did a single one of these rise above the noise level to make its voice—and its plea—heard?

Feeling confused and a little overwhelmed, Nell pushed herself up from the laptop and wandered to the Aga where she stirred the soup, then absently and experimentally, added a teaspoon of savory.

Still considering, she reached for the jar of fennel, the addition of which required the extra step of toasting several tablespoonsful of the seeds. Nell dug out the immersion blender and treated the soup to a thorough scrounging. Soup and Kernow's story whirled together.

A light was shining from Bunty Whitney's studio. When she was deeply involved in building a pot, Bunty often lost track of time and forgot to eat. Nell filled a deep bowl—in fact one of Bunty's own hand-thrown artifacts—balanced the sour cream container on top and stuffed the sherry bottle under her arm. Then she slipped out her back door and crossed the lawn to her backdoor neighbor's property.

Bunty opened the studio door, looking cross. She didn't like interruptions. Nell understood this. She didn't appreciate them either.

"You need to eat." Nell was blunt. "And I," she continued, stepping over the sill, "need a break and some company."

She regarded her neighbor with affection. Bunty was wearing a long cotton skirt, woolen stockings and worn L.L. Bean camp moccasins. Her hair was coming unpinned. Clay had leached the oils from Bunty's hands and left them wrinkled and dry, the cuticles clay-encrusted.

"Ummm," Bunty's crossness evaporated as she leaned over the bowl to sniff deeply. "What kind?"

"Vitamin-charged split-pea. I super-charged it with fresh spinach—enough to power Popeye. What's *your* project du jour?"

Nell drew the bottle of sherry from under her arm, but Bunty proposed a glass of wine before they tucked into the soup. Then, with balloon glasses of red wine in hand, they viewed the line of somewhat lumpy plates that Bunty had under construction.

"I'm trying to make a full set," Bunty sighed, "but, I don't know, maybe I'll just consign the whole lot to the bin and go back to making mugs."

She looked gloomy. But then, brightening, she turned to Nell. "How 'bout you? How's your project coming?"

"A bit like yours ," Nell confessed. "Lumpy. I'm running into some frustrations, but I can't really explain what they are or why I'm feeling this way. So the hell with it for now!"

She lifted her glass.

"I'll drink to that!" seconded Bunty, smacking her glass against Nell's so vigorously that Nell was surprised when the balloon glasses didn't shatter.

Nell slathered the pea soup into a pair of soup plates. She splashed a jigger of sherry into each and drew a table knife through the soup for a marbling affect and added a generous dollop of sour cream to each.

"Fit for two aging beauties," Bunty declared with satisfaction. And she tucked in.

SOUPED-UP SPLIT-PEA SOUP

2 teaspoons of olive oil
1 russet potato, peeled and diced
1 sweet potato, peeled and diced
2 carrots, coarsely chopped
1 yellow onion, coarsely chopped
1 cup dried split peas, sorted and rinsed
6 cups of chicken stock
1 pound of spinach, washed and torn into pieces, stems removed
Salt and pepper to taste
1 jigger of dry sherry per serving
1 tablespoon of sour cream per serving.

Heat the olive oil and start sautéing the onion and carrots, then add the potatoes, and cook until the vegetables are softened. Stir in the chicken stock and the peas. Bring to the boil, then simmer partially covered until all the vegetables—especially the peas—are tender. Add the seasonings and add more liquid (either water or stock) if needed. Stir in the torn spinach and cook for 5 or 10 more minutes. Ladle into flat soup plates and pour the sherry around on top. Using a kitchen knife, swirl the sherry. Top with a tablespoon of sour cream.

~

Chapter 11

"The book isn't an autobiography, of course," Nell was saying. "It's an adventure story—specifically, a story of a life-changing event. Nevertheless, it's important to know more about your background. Ultimately, this may be important only to me—we'll see—but I do want to have a clear understanding of where David Kernow came from and what events shaped him into the man he is."

"Sure," Deke said. "Sounds reasonable. Although there's really not much to tell."

And apparently there wasn't. Deke's recollections were as curt as entries on a resume. A much less effusive client sat across the table from Nell this morning. In fact, Deke seemed to have no enthusiasm for the subject.

"I was an only child."

Nell waited. The point where a narrator begins a story had always been revealing to Nell. She watched Deke collect his thoughts.

"My mother died when I was fourteen—some kind of complication from a liver disorder. Within six months my father remarried."

Deke stopped again, and Nell waited some more.

"My father—my old man—was a cold bastard. He was successful and proud of his success. He'd started a company—Kernow Industries—and he ran the business like it was San Quentin and he was the warden. He made a lot of money, but I don't think his employees liked him much. They may have respected him, but I think he scared them to death. He was a Type A-plus guy with a workaholic's ethic. He worked nineteen hours out of twenty-four, and I think he resented the five hours that he wasn't working because he was sleeping."

Nell saw a hard knot appear at the hinge of Kernow's jaw.

"What about your stepmother? Did you get along with her?"

"Her name was Grace," Deke said, "and the name didn't suit her. She was the least graceful or gracious person I've ever known. She owned a real estate firm and she worked about as hard as he did. Grace Didrickson. She never did take his name."

There was another spell of silence while Deke seemed to consider Grace. He cleared the memory with a shake of his head.

"We lived in Hamilton. That's where I grew up. Lived in a big house off Bay Road. Prep school was Josiah Palmer—predictably. Good college prep school. The Old Man was hell-bound and determined I'd go to MIT, as he had, and he made sure the faculty at Palmer hit all the marks that would drop-kick me right through the front door."

In the silence that followed this recollection, Nell quietly dropped a question.

"If you'd had a choice, would it have been MIT?"

Deke seemed startled, like he'd never entertained the question.

"I—I don't know. It wasn't a consideration."

"You're describing a pretty austere set of circumstances. Weren't you lonely?"

"I don't know. Probably. I did have my grandmother though." He chuckled reminiscently. "Myrtle. Myrtle Mapes Kernow of

Magnolia, Massachusetts. Have you ever heard of her?'

Nell indicated she had not.

"Well, she was a quite a character around Magnolia. A lot of people knew her by sight and reputation if not by introduction. She drove a roadster. And she didn't drive it well. She charged along like Toad of Toad Hall with the top down and the wind in her white curls, bumping up and down over curbs—where there were curbs anyhow. Otherwise she just ran over people's lawns. When she couldn't find the horn, she'd holler out 'Toot! Toot!' then laugh like mad at her own silliness. She was insanely happy and fun to be around. She was generous, and she was very good to me. I loved to go to Magnolia!"

"Did you call her Grammy?"

Deke laughed. "Hell, no! I called her Myrtle Mapes. Everyone did, including my late grandfather apparently. I never met him."

"Is that what your father called her too?"

"Hardly!" Deke snorted. "He called her 'Mother', and he made it sound it like a swear word. He didn't approve of Myrtle Mapes."

"So Myrtle Mapes was your father's mother?"

"Yes, and I never understood how she could have hatched such a hard-boiled egg. They used to argue, and Myrtle Mapes was the only person I ever saw get the better of my old man."

"Okay," Nell decided to move the story along. "You got into MIT, obviously. What was that like? What did you study?"

"Electrical engineering. The Old Man figured a double E would take me just about anywhere I wanted to go and would be a base to branch out as innovations came along. Turns out he was right." Deke added grudgingly, "I'll grant him that much anyway."

"So what was college like?"

"Well, for openers, I was away from home. For the first time, other than an occasional overnight in Magnolia with Myrtle Mapes, I was away and on my own. That was like drinking fresh water when you're unbearably thirsty. Like opening a window in a hot attic and letting in fresh air."

He laughed at some internal amusement.

"I had this roommate—John Altman—he was from Chicago and he was great! We got up to some wild old times, I can tell you. Pretty much tore up Cambridge. Boston too. Irish pubs in the South End. Girls from Radcliffe. I bought a car at the end of the first semester and then we'd drive out the pike and pick up girls from Smith and Mount Holyoke. Smokin' times."

He shook his head appreciatively.

"What did you study?"

"Study? This and that. Turned serious after freshman year though. Altman's folks told him if he didn't buckle down he'd either lose his scholarship or they'd bounce him out. So we kind of went our own ways sophomore year. We stayed in touch though. Still do."

"And after college?"

"The Navy. I applied to the SEALs. Got accepted. It's something I'm quite proud of actually, but I don't talk about much. I got hurt. Injured on a maneuver and so that ended that part of my CV."

"And then?"

"Then." Deke passed his hand over his face. "Let's see. First marriage, first start-up. Second marriage, second start-up."

He suddenly laughed.

"Are you seeing a pattern here? Hey. I told you I started up three companies, and I'll be happy to go into each, but let's call it a day right here, okay? Three companies, three marriages, a lot of money."

"So are you married presently?"

"Yes."

"Your third wife."

"Correct."

Nell raised her eyebrows encouragingly but Deke didn't accept her invitation to speak about the third Mrs. Kernow or any of her predecessors.

"Three marriages, one horrific tragedy and a new life," he summarized. "Shall we make a date for next time?"

Nell quietly shut her notebook and pressed the Sony's stop button.

"That will be just fine," she said.

Three-quarters of an hour after the session started, Nell was surprised to find herself sitting in her car in Kernow's driveway. He'd dispensed with the first two decades of his life in under an hour. What, Nell wondered, could that mean?

∾

Chapter 12

Nell had snagged a booth in Angie's and hunched there, trying to warm her cold fingers on a mug of hot coffee, was feeling guilty. Angie's was crowded, and people waiting for seats were starting to give her dirty looks. Like, it's a booth for *four*, honey. Get it? Nell kept her eyes down and silently cursed Robert and Jerry for being so late.

Outside, Angie's windows streamed with rain and inside they were fogged with steam from breakfasts being cooked and people huffing to cool their coffee.

At last! There they were! Nell's arm shot up involuntarily. They saw her and pushed through the clot of waiting breakfasters toward her table—tall, bespectacled Robert looking dignified and shorter, ginger-haired Jerry beaming with undisguised pleasure.

"Nellybean!" exclaimed Jerry, "Delicious to see you!"

"Sorry," said Robert. "Parking."

Jerry took the bench across from Nell, sliding over to leave room for Robert.

"I am famished!" he declared. "This one drove at the speed limit all the way while I was *dying* for a coffee and a real fry-up."

"Coffee for you guys?" The waitress materialized, gestured

62

with her carafe and slammed two mugs on the table. She was wearing a tee shirt that said Angie's.

"We can order whenever you're ready," Jerry told her.

"Right."

She poured the coffee, topped off Nell's mug, and pulled the order pad out of a back pocket of her jeans. Nell, helpless to do otherwise, counted the young woman's piercings. While Jerry's extensive order was written up, she counted her rings. She was about to start counting the woman's bangle bracelets, but Robert's order was short.

"Oatmeal, please."

"You're just having oatmeal?"

"Why? What's wrong with oatmeal?"

Jerry shook his head.

The waitress looked at Nell. "You?"

"One egg, please—sunnyside up—with wheat toast and an orange juice."

"Fresh or otherwise?"

"Oh, fresh, please," said Nell

"I wonder what otherwise is," mused Jerry when the waitress left. "Unfresh? Stale?"

"They actually squeeze the oranges here," Nell told him. "It's expensive but it is a scrumptious luxury."

Good heavens, she thought, I'm talking like Jerry. But when the food came, Jerry was quick to order a fresh orange juice also.

Conversation through breakfast was of the rain, Boston traffic, the Red Sox who were doing their best to disappoint fans again this year, and the latest scandal on Beacon Hill. Then Jerry placed his knife and fork precisely across his empty plate.

"Well, I'll leave you two to talk amongst yourselves," he said. "Let me out, darling."

Robert obligingly stood so Jerry could slide across the bench.

"Meet you at the bookstore on State Street in three-quarters of an hour?" Jerry raised his eyebrows at them.

"Check," Robert told him. And to Nell he added, "Jerry's dying to go through the shops on State Street. He regards it as a fact-gathering, business trip."

"Ah, knowing what to steal and when to steal it," Jerry tapped his finger on the side of his nose, "it's all in the instinct."

He slapped a waterproof scally cap on his head and headed into the rain, bound for retail reconnaissance.

"So?" Robert said. "Does he have a real book attached to his 9/11 drama?"

"I'm gathering material industriously," Nell told him. "Deke is very forthcoming about some things and apparently quite reticent about others. What do you know about Children of Woe?"

"Been to a fund-raiser. Big house out in Carlisle. About seventy-five people milling, drinking, chatting each other up."

"You contributed?"

"Sure. A hundred dollars to shuffle up to Carlisle for champagne cocktails and a catered buffet."

"Was Deke there?"

"Oh, very much the host. Jovial. Solicitous. He's clearly a people person."

"Did you meet the third Mrs. Kernow?"

Robert considered.

"Um, yes—yes, I did. Typical trophy wife. Big hair. Christian Lauboutin sling-backs."

"You remember her *shoes*?"

"Yeah, those red-soled things. $745 a pair. Jerry told me."

"My god," Nell told herself. Nell's idea of dressy shoes was Nine West sandals.

She tried tapping another reservoir.

"What about Myrtle Mapes? Ever heard of her?'

"Who?"

"Myrtle Mapes Kernow."

"No. Can't say I have."

"You probably wouldn't unless you were from Gloucester. Deke's grandmother."

"His grandmother," Robert repeated thoughtfully. "Hmm. So where do you go from here?"

"On, I guess," said Nell. "Keep vacuuming up details. Writing drafts. Seeing what I can shake out of Kernow and seeing what I can do with what shakes out."

Robert looked at his watch.

"Jerry'll be waiting for us. Unless he got loose inside Red Bird Trading Co. and fell through time."

~

Chapter 13

"I hope you're prepared to snow me under with details about those three start-ups," Nell smiled. She placed the Sony recorder on Deke's table. "So. Tell me stories."

Deke pushed back in his chair. He clasped his hands behind his head and, arms akimbo, launched into the apparently pleasurable task of storytelling.

"Let's see. Start at the beginning, I guess. Charlie Carney was a consummate engineer—black, horn-rimmed glasses, a pocket protector with about nine pens sprouting out of it, and a ring of keys jangling from his belt loop. In school, he always had a slide rule dangling off his belt. I think he wore it even after slide rules grew passé and he'd upgraded to a Bowmar calculator. Charlie was conservative, you see."

Deke helped himself to a laugh, thinking apparently of Charlie Carney

"Charlie had no social graces whatsoever. He was a back-room guy—a guy who tinkered at a bench and who wanted nothing more from life except to tinker at a bench wiring and soldering components onto breadboards. And he tinkered day and night— far into the night."

Nell watched Deke's eyes drift out of focus as he rewound his memory.

"Somebody told me years later that Charlie had gotten married, and I was never so surprised by anything in my life. But that's just an aside."

Deke returned to his story.

"The SemiConsolidated Systems story—SemiConsolidated being the first start-up—begins with Charlie Carney."

"You probably don't need to know this part," Deke told Nell. "But I'll give just a little technical background so you have a handle on how Charlie spent his time. Semiconductors are the foundation of modern electronics. Before they were developed, it was all vacuum tubes. Anyhow, the current in a semiconductor comes either from free electrons or from "holes". These are known as charge carriers and the number of charge carriers in a semi can be modified by doping. That is, by introducing small amounts of impurity atoms. When a semi has an excess of "holes", we call it a "p-type"; when there's an excess of atoms, it's an "n-type". So old Charlie is at his bench working out the highly controlled conditions that allow for the increasingly precise control of p-and n-type dopants. You see?"

Nell didn't. However she tapped a finger on the Sony.

"Not really," she admitted, "but I have everything you're explaining right here. When I've written a draft, you can check it over and we'll work on a rewrite so it will be correct."

"Okay. So a guy like Charlie Carney needs a partner who is also technical—someone who understands what the hell is going on—therefore that partner has to be a technical guy like me. And secondly, he needs someone to market the stuff he's developing. Someone like me. Oh, and thirdly, Charlie needed capital. Once again—me."

Deke tapped his chest in satisfaction.

"So I threw my lot in with Charlie Carney, and I did

development and marketing and schmoozed and sold product and built a name and a customer base for SemiConsolidated. Meanwhile, Charlie futzed with dopants and manipulated holes and electrons and worked on gaining a respectable product. And that went on for some years."

Deke stopped, tipped forward in his chair, and laid his forearms on the table.

"And then what happened," Nell prompted. "What happened to the company?"

"For me, not much. I went on to a second start-up—Kernow Light—my LED outfit. LEDs were a natural evolution out of semiconductor-based electronics—hence Kernow Light."

"You started it with Charlie?"

"No, Charlie and I went our separate ways at that point. I'd grown bored with SemiConsolidated. Felt I'd done all I could for the company. So Charlie bought out my share of the business and I threw the whole magilla into Kernow Light."

"Did you have a partner?"

"A sort of minority partner. Actually he had the title of chief engineer. Jules Stutzman. He was kind of a bastard. Had a terrible personality—a really nasty streak—but he knew what he was doing as far as LED technology went, so we moved into some warehouse space in Beverly and went into business."

"Were you successful?"

"Sure." Deke grinned. "Would you doubt it?"

"So what happened to Kernow Light?" Nell wanted to know.

"Two things, basically. Stutzman wanted a bigger piece of the pie. Actually, he wanted the whole pie, and he went about getting it in underhanded ways. Going around my back to customers and suppliers, even to the technical media. Damn near ruined my reputation. He had the ethics of a slumlord. I couldn't deal with that. The other thing was—again—boredom. I was ready for greener pastures. So Jules and I parted company."

"But the company had your name," Nell pointed out, protesting.

"Yeah. Well. Stutzman kept the name for a while, and then he changed it as soon as he could. I think he merged with another outfit and they started calling themselves something-something. Some word that was a blend of their two names. It wasn't very memorable; as you can see, I can't even recall it."

"So did you leave with a handsome bundle of money?"

"Not as handsome as I'd have liked—or as I deserved. Stutzman had done a lot of damage behind my back and things got decidedly ugly."

Deke gestured as if he were waving away unpleasant cigarette smoke.

"The less said the better," he concluded.

"And then?"

"Then? Then Compu-Savvy. It was the beginning of the dot-com era. And I got in on the ground floor. What a roller-coaster ride! But it was fun. Exciting! At least for a while."

Deke smiled reminiscently.

"So you participated in the dot-com debacle," Nell said with a small, qualified smile. "Tell me about that."

"Well, Compu-Savvy had its roots in computer signal processing, but eventually expanded into a fleet of computational products all poised to deliver "fast math" solutions. It was 1995 when we established Compu-Savvy. We rode the business up like it was an elevator and we went public. Two MIT guys organized the start-up—Chuck Bennett and Craig Craddock—and they invited me in. My job was development and venture capital. In other words, use my not inconsiderable connections to bring in money."

Deke was silent for a few minutes. Nell was patient.

"In 1998 the stock hit $98 a share. That plummeted to $9 a share when the tech stock bubble collapsed in 2000. The company lost a large chunk of market capitalization in the collapse, but still, we were able to hold Compu-Savvy's corporate nose above waves, and I'm happy to say that the company eventually regained stability and profitability. It never went completely under—I mean some dot-coms failed completely. Zero. That's all she wrote. Compu-Savvy hung on, and its stock eventually surpassed that 1998 level."

"But you're not part of the company now?" Nell put in.

"No," Deke said. "For me, Compu-Savvy ended with 9/11. I chucked over my share of the business after the Towers went down. I hadn't the stomach for any of it any longer. Took what little money I got from the deal—remember the stock at that point hadn't come all the way back. It was starting to regain some ground but was a long way from that 1998 high. I sucked up the loss and put everything I had into starting up The Children of Woe Fund."

Deke fell silent again and Nell didn't interrupt him. She was thinking about the work ahead of her. Thinking about digesting the information that the Sony now held. She would have to write very carefully, and Deke would have to check and edit her drafts.

"Any more?" she asked.

Her client regarded her. "Not for now," he said. "Let's see how this turns out.

Nell tapped off the Sony and stood to leave. Deke held the study door for her and ushered her into the foyer just as the front door opened. A woman in tennis whites, key in hand, stood there.

"This is Nell Bane, sweetie, the woman who is writing my book. Nell, this is my wife."

The third Mrs. Kernow—Deke had not offered her name— had good teeth, a good tan and probably a good cleavage when it was displayed in the sort of dress designed to look well in photos at fund-raisers and charitable events.

The third Mrs. Kernow stretched her mouth to a width that could be taken for a smile, although her eyes didn't join the effort.

"Pleased to meet you," she murmured as she brushed past and hurried down the hall in the direction of the kitchen,

"Yes," Nell said weakly, turning to watch her go. "As am I."

∼

Chapter 14

Nell could feel a cold coming on. Her standard treatment for colds included rest, aspirin, warm socks, and massive doses of hot-sour soup—old-fashioned Jewish penicillin enhanced with enough hot red pepper to sear a sore throat and steam open stuffed sinuses. She had the necessary chicken stock in the freezer, of course, and there were dried mushrooms and even a can of bamboo shoots in the pantry, but the soup would require fresh tofu and a small purple turnip as well as some of that red-rimmed Chinese pork. Feeling too unwell to forage about the grocery store, she simply took herself to the local Chinese restaurant for a double take-out order of Mr. Chang's hot-sour soup. Mr. Chang handed over the soup with a sympathetic smile and a word of instruction.

"Feel bettah soon, Missy Bane."

"Thank you, Mr. Chang. You keep yourself and your family away from this cold bug."

Her homemade recipe could wait for another day.

HOT-SOUR SOUP FOR ANOTHER DAY
6 cups of chicken stock
1 cup of water

1/4 cup purple turnip, shredded
1/2 cup shredded Chinese pork
1/2 cup canned bamboo shoots, drained and finely chopped
1/2 cup dried mushrooms, whatever kind you can find in the grocery
1 cake of tofu, patted dry and sliced into matchsticks
Dried red pepper flakes, 1 teaspoon or to taste
1/4 cup cider vinegar
1-1/2 tablespoons soy sauce
2 teaspoons of cornstarch

On another day, Nell would combine the vinegar, soy sauce and cornstarch and set the mixture aside. Then she'd reconstitute the mushrooms in a cup of hot water and let them bathe for 30 minutes before draining and discarding the mushrooms water.

When the chicken stock and water were brought to a boil in a large pot and then had simmered for 5 minutes, the turnip, pork, bamboo and drained mushrooms would be stirred in and simmered. After 5 minutes, in would go the tofu and red pepper and when the soup was just at the boil, the cornstarch mixture would be added to thicken the soup slightly, and for the next to 20 minutes the hot-sour soup would chuckle away to itself at the simmer.

It was an unpleasant cold, but at least it didn't feature a nasty cough. Nell was prepared, though, if it had. Her remedy was whiskey, lemon and honey—a tablespoonful at bedtime.

Meanwhile she listened to the Sony play the stories of Deke Kernow's three start-ups and entertained disturbing dreams about semiconductors, light emiting diodes and dot-coms.

∼

Chapter 15

Rocky Neck shoves itself out into Gloucester's Inner Harbor, tethered to the town by a skinny strip of land named, or misnamed, Rocky Harbor Ave. The road can't be traveled above fifteen miles an hour and an avenue it certainly isn't. The Neck's east side shelters the part of the harbor known as Smith's Cove, and it was on this Cove side that Nell located the offices of Children of Woe. She doubled back and parked in the town lot, then made her way along the street—a pleasant walk actually—that took her past small art galleries and studios, most with tiny, enticing gardens. From Madfish Grill, the smell of frying broadcast the promise of lunch over the entire Neck.

The address written on Nell's scrap of paper delivered her to a structure that looked unpromising—a steep, shingled building that seemed to have been painted with creosote. Still, there was a small nameplate that announced The Children of Woe Fund, so Nell entered and climbed a flight of wooden stairs that indicated several centuries of feet had preceded her.

The single door at the top of the stairs was half-glassed—the old-fashioned pocked and bubbled glass that admitted only the dimmest light. Bathroom glass Nell's mother had called it. She knocked. Then knocked again. The sense of foreboding that had settled on her like dust when she stepped inside the dark foyer downstairs increased a few degrees.

"Come in," called a distant female voice.

Nell did so and drew in a sharp breath of surprise.

The entire wall on the harbor side had been replaced with glass. Sun pennies shot starbursts off the water. Blue sky that seemed to stretch into eternity, turned the water beneath actually blue. Nell took in the gray rocks banking the wharves and jetties, the white sails of a few pleasure craft, and the black iron of cranes that did the harbor's work.

Nell stood and stared. She slowly became aware of a woman watching her.

"Oh! Sorry," Nell said. "I was just taken by surprise by the—by all the light and—and everything."

The woman nodded but did not smile.

"It happens," she said.

"Well, I'm Nell Bane." Nell activated her most charming smile as she stepped toward the woman. She hoped it was charming anyway. "I have an appointment with Mr. Kernow."

"He's not here."

"Oh. Then perhaps I'm a little early. He is expected, I assume?"

The question was answered with a shrug.

Nell was disconcerted.

"Do you mind if I wait—wait a while and see if he—if he comes?"

"Help yourself."

Nell looked around. There was a sofa against the inner wall flanked by a pair of chairs and a grouping of armchairs closer to the windows, arranged with a view of the harbor. Nell strayed rather casually in the direction of the view. She decided to try again for rapport.

"You're Mr. Kernow's administration assistant, I would gather?

Would you be Ms. Morrissey?"

An exaggerated sigh was followed by the act of ostentatiously placing a pencil on the desk, perfectly parallel to the top edge.

"Yes. I am Patricia Morrissey."

"I see. Thank you."

Nell turned back toward the view, determined to ask no more questions.

"Miss Dry Ice," she said under her breath.

Well, she'd give it ten minutes, she decided. After that, if Deke hadn't arrived, she'd leave. She was aware of time passing. Patricia Morrissey worked at her desk with her head down.

Ten minutes. Time was up. Nell decided to give it another five. When time ran out for the second time, she stood and addressed Ms. Morrissey's back.

"I think I'll just..."

The door burst open. Deke seemed to absorb all the air when he exploded into the room.

"Nell! So sorry. Gosh! Traffic. Good to see you. Did you make yourself comfortable? Did my secretary offer you coffee?"

"Oh, I'm fine," Nell said quickly. "Coffee wasn't necessary."

Patricia Morrissey had stopped working and was watching them neutrally.

"Administrative assistant," she said.

"Whatever," Deke answered. Then, in a warmer tone he again addressed Nell. "Well, I'm having coffee! What'll you have? How do you take it?"

"Black," replied Nell. "Very simple."

"Patty!" Deke directed, "Two coffees, one black, one light with two sugars."

He did not, Nell noted, say please. When Miss Dry Ice returned with two paper cups, Deke did not acknowledge her.

"Thank you." Nell smiled up at the young woman. Patty's Morrissey's expression did not change.

Over the rim of his coffee cup, Deke was smiling at her.

"So whaddaya think of the place?"

"The view is spectacular. A charming blend of vintage industrial and contemporary elegance."

Deke seemed gratified by the description.

"Thought you didn't like mid-century."

"I don't call this mid-century. I'd call it industrial chic."

"Well, we aren't here to discuss design," Deke concluded. "You wanted to see the Children of Woe headquarters and this is it."

"So what goes on here?"

"This is Command Central," Deke said casually. "Correspondence goes in and out. Invitations to fund raisers are organized, collated and sent from here. Social media, of course, is big. Patty sends a couple Tweets each day and manages the Fund's Facebook and LinkedIn pages. And Ira Zayder is in several times a week to handle the financial stuff. Patty also logs in checks, does general bookkeeping."

Nell glanced over at Miss Dry Ice who didn't seem to be paying any attention.

"I'd like to meet Ira Zayder," she said.

"As I said, he's not here everyday." Deke raised his voice, "Patty! When is Ira in?"

"Tuesdays and Thursdays," she replied without lifting her eyes from her work. "Afternoons usually. Sometimes Fridays."

"May I make an appointment with him?" Nell asked her.

The Fund's administrative assistant slowly raised her eyes and looked at Nell.

"Certainly. Would you like me to set one up?"

"Please," said Nell. "I would appreciate it very much."

She crossed the room and placed her card on the desk. Patty Morrissey picked up the card and read it. Nell had the impression she was even reading the phone numbers and addresses in seven-point type.

"I'll email you."

"I'd be grateful."

She turned to Deke. "It helps very much to be able to visualize settings, so when I write this part of the story, I will now know how the offices look and feel. I'll have absorbed some of the atmosphere. Thank you for showing this magnificent view to me."

She turned to Patty Morrissey.

"And thank you too—for the coffee and for ..."

Nell waved her hand helplessly.

"Well ... for setting up the appointment. Thanks."

As Nell closed the office door and prepared to put her foot on the first worn step, she heard Deke's voice erupt from the other side of the door.

"Patty! Goddam it! What'd you do with those papers from Barringer?"

Patty Morrissey's answer was a mumble Nell couldn't hear.

With her hand on the rail, she descended quickly.

～

Chapter 16

Instead of heading back toward Route 128, Nell decided to detour through the center of Gloucester and exit through the town's Magnolia section.

The local color was at its most colorful in Gloucester, and the stop-start traffic gave Nell the opportunity to take in the scene of salty bars—the hang-outs of fishermen stopping briefly off the boats—that stood elbow-to-elbow with chic little bistros, vintage clothing stores and upscale shops purveying exotic vinegars, olive oil and jewelry. Down the hill and directly on the water, boatyards were brisk with business and Gorton's fish processing plant, the new modern one, was in full throttle. Nell, traveling slowly out of the Center, passed the famous statue of the Gloucester fisherman and felt the traffic congestion unlock.

Still in her sponge mode and ready to absorb more impressions, Nell cruised into the area known as Magnolia, Massachusetts, home of Deke's grandmother, the late Myrtle Mapes Kernow. She rolled slowly around the neighborhood, staring at the houses and trying to imagine which one might have belonged to Myrtle Mapes. Which house might have been a safe haven for one lonely young boy?

With no answers, Nell drove on until she could hitch onto 133 and drive north through Essex, through Ipswich, through Rowley and finally, onto Route 1 and the old bridge over the marshes of Newbury. Then it was Newburyport at last. Home.

Nell sat at the kitchen counter, typing her impressions into the laptop. The ancient building, the mid-blowing view, Miss Dry Ice and Deke's less-than-gentlemanly treatment of her spun out in detail under Nell's flying fingers. She paused at that last one. This was a side of David Kernow's personality that was unexpected. She had never seen him as anything but a genial fellow, eager to please. She decided she'd need to see more of the Children of Woe headquarters and the people who climbed those ancient stairs every day.

~

Chapter 17

"Well, I asked for this," Nell murmured, scolding herself.

Her closet door was open and she'd been leaning on it for quite some time. What did you wear to a fund-raiser? Rather, what did you wear if you were Nell Bane and spent most of your time in jeans and baggy sweaters? She had a few dresses, of course, but since she didn't attend many fund-raisers (had she ever been to one?) appropriate choices were limited.

Nell made a point of looking at the photographs from fund-raisers that appeared in *North Shore Magazine* and *Boston Magazine*. For some reason she read each caption avidly, squinting at the miniscule type, although she rarely recognized the individuals pictured there. They always looked like they were having fun, though, Nell had noticed that. Looked like they were having one helluva good time.

"Serves me right," she said now. "Should have kept my big mouth shut."

In the interests of color-gathering, she had asked Deke if she could attend a Children of Woe event. He had been delighted. By coincidence, there was one coming up right there in Lexington, and he'd be pleased to have Nell as his guest.

But no. If Nell were to attend, she insisted on contributing. She wanted to be on equal footing with the other guests, not there as a paid hack or a charity case. So she'd ponied up the hundred-dollar head charge and written her personal check to The Children of Woe Fund. That would be tax deductible, of course, but the dress she'd have to buy wouldn't be. In the end, though, Nell decided on the little black cocktail dress that had been to numerous Christmas parties and open houses around Newburyport. It was slender, long-sleeved, and had a neckline that didn't plunge to the depths usually seen in the magazine photos, but it wasn't a turtleneck either. You couldn't go wrong with an LBD, Nell always thought.

Shoes. Well, the Nine West black sandals would have to do. Christian Lauboutin was out of the question.

The fund-raiser was being hosted in a converted barn just a few blocks west of Lexington Center. The barn loomed above a wide, curved driveway, but Nell, fearing entrapment by the cars of late-arriving guests—someone was forever blocking her in, then settling down to party-hearty late into the night—drove past the address and parked the Saab on the street. This meant she had to pick her way along the dark sidewalk on her perilous Nine West high-heeled sandals. Her feet were freezing by the time she arrived at the barn door, but at least she hadn't fallen down and ripped the knees out of her pantyhose. She had just located the rope that hung from an old farm bell, when the door swung wide revealing her effusive host.

"In! In!" he cried. "Come in!"

And Nell was swept into this stranger's embrace, peeled out of her coat and handed a glass of something pale and bubbly. It looked like Champagne but at the first sip, Nell decided it probably wasn't.

To get the lay of the land, Nell stood near a wall and inventoried her surroundings. The barn, formerly the property of the house next door, had been renovated and great care had been taken not to obscure the fact that this had, indeed, been a barn. The renovation, Nell decided, had not been made with sensitivity. As a result, the great room, in which the party was already surging, was cavernous. The acoustics were horrifying; the room had the din of a gymnasium.

Nell mingled. She introduced herself, learned names, asked discrete questions, kept her observations sharp, and memorized facts and impressions as fast as she could. The fund-raisers' hosts, she learned, were a youngish and terribly hip couple from New York, eager to embrace all things New England and to blend at warp-speed with the locals. They seemed unaware that they hadn't blended and would never be mistaken for natives.

Nell eventually identified her hostess—a tall woman who was dancing a sort of fandango between clots of guests, the kitchen, and the drinks table and who, while she did this, managed to keep laughing, talking, and inquiring solicitously of her guests whether all needs were being met. Nell edged toward her and introduced herself.

"I'm Diane!" the hostess declared, pumping Nell's hand enthusiastically. "So you're writing Deke's story! How marvelous!"

Nell couldn't think how to respond to that, so she quickly smiled broadly.

"I know you're busy, but could I just ask you a couple of questions?"

"Of course, darling! Ask away!"

Diane, Nell noted, seemed to specialize in unspoken exclamation points.

"Well, I'd like to know how you know Deke, and then how you came to be doing this fund-raiser."

Diane grew even more animated. Apparently Nell's interest delighted her.

"Is this for the book?"

"Well, it could be," Nell hedged. "I am trying to learn about the people who are drawn to support The Children of Woe Fund."

"We, that is Kenny and I, attended a fund-raiser much like this one. Someone we knew was having one. We met Deke there and were very impressed, both with him and with his cause. It's such a worthy cause, don't you think?"

Here, Diane placed a hand on Nell's forearm and leaned toward her earnestly.

Nell, in turn, leaned toward Diane and just as earnestly agreed.

Satisfied with the validation, Diane continued her tale.

"Well, bottom line, Kenny and I decided we'd also like to host a fund-raiser."

"And just what does that entail?" Nell wanted to know.

"The Children of Woe staff—and Deke I suppose—supply a guest list. They send out invitations, then let us know the number of people who will be attending. We," she gestured expansively with her drink, indicating the surroundings, "supply the venue and the catering and drinks. That's our contribution."

Nell looked around.

"So, what would you say? How many in attendance?"

Diane pursed her lips in thought. "Well, eighty-seven people responded that they'd be here. I doubt that quite that number has shown up. Don't you find that some people RSVP in the affirmative and then blow it off?"

Nell, who had never found that, nodded quickly, and with terrier-like determination, pursued her tack.

"That's quite a generous contribution," she said. "Providing food and drink for that number."

"It is for a worthy cause," said Diane in an exalted tone, "and besides, Kenny and I just love a good party. We have the space for it, you know."

A young woman wearing a black dress and a worried pucker on her forehead appeared at Diane's elbow and whispered urgently.

"Oh, oh! Of course," the hostess whispered back. And to Nell she said, "So sorry. Must dash. Slight emergency in the kitchen."

Nell strolled on.

David Kernow was very much in evidence. A pod of people surrounded him—indeed, moved with him—like a school of pilot fish grouped around a whale. When he took a step, the contingent shifted en mass.

"Nell!" He spotted her and waved extravagantly over the heads of the pilot fish, who turned as one to stare. Deke pushed through the school and reached Nell, bending to kiss her cheek in greeting.

"Having fun?"

"Yes," Nell replied. "Absolutely. It looks like a marvelous turn-out. Is this about what these events draw?"

Deke looked around him as if seeing his guests for the first time. "Yeah. Maybe a few less than expected, but—hey!—the night is still young. What're you drinking?"

Nell stared at her glass as if seeing it for the first time. The level was considerably reduced although she couldn't remember sipping much. She drank very little at parties, knowing she'd be her own designated driver. A glass was mostly a prop—something to hold and to signal conviviality. If you didn't have a drink, someone was always insisting on fetching you one.

"I don't know. Something pale."

"Here." Deke lifted a new glass off a passing tray and handed it to Nell who found herself awkwardly holding two glasses. She'd have to find a sneaky spot to ditch a glass.

"Who do you want to meet?" Deke asked. "Rather, whom."

He looked pleased with himself.

"I was really hoping to see Ira Zayder. Patty Morrissey seems to be having some trouble setting up our meeting."

"Oh, Ira doesn't come to these things," Deke told her blandly. "He's an introvert. That's a polite way of saying he's antisocial. Sorry. I guess you'll have to keep working with Patty on that."

A tall woman with earrings dangling to her shoulders, squeezed Deke's arm and took that as an opportunity to press her breasts into him.

"Ah," Deke said. "The very person! Helene Porter, meet Nell Bane—she's helping me write my story. Going to make me famous. Going to take me all the way to Hollywood, aren't you Nell? Helene, I want you to talk to Nell. Tell her all about your interest in Children of Woe."

Helene turned to regard Nell without enthusiasm. Her prey—Deke Kernow—had just slipped her snare and was off across the room, and here she was stuck with this nondescript woman in the little black dress.

Nell smiled at Helene apologetically.

"Have you known Deke long?"

"Just since the Towers went down, really. My husband Gordon and I were so affected that we wanted to do something. We were casting about, really. And then we were introduced to Deke and it was wonderful, really. We could donate our money to a terrific cause with the assurance that the money would go almost directly to the children of the victims. There was no middleman, really. No costly overhead. And Deke is wonderful! Brilliant! Amazing!"

"Does Gordon think he's amazing too?"

Helene threw Nell a sharp look to see if she was being put on, but Nell looked innocent.

"Yes," said Helene tersely. "He does."

"Is Gordon here?"

Helene looked around as if she weren't sure whether they'd come together or not, and—if they had—she couldn't remember where she'd misplaced him.

"Over there."

With a jerk of her head, Helene indicated a man seated in a club chair in the shadows under a former haymow.

Since this information seemed to have concluded their

conversation, Helene moved away to stalk Deke further and Nell, with a straying sort of sideways motion, made for the club chair and Gordon. He was staring straight ahead, focused on nothing in particular.

"Good evening," Nell said rather hesitantly.

Gordon, using his entire head, swiveled to look up at her.

"I was rather envying you," Nell told him, "sitting over here out of the traffic but still where you can see all the action."

She smiled. Gordon did not.

"I was just introduced to your wife," Nell told him. "I understand you and she come to these fund-raisers quite often."

Gordon sighed. "Yeah. Often. Helene enjoys them. Makes her feel like Lady Bountiful and she gets to rub elbows and shoulders and other parts with *fas*-cinating people."

Nell laughed. "Do you not find them fascinating as well?"

Gordon sighed again. "Oh, they're alright, I suppose. I'd just rather be home with a history book, a lap robe and a small glass of brandy."

He looked up at Nell apologetically, "I'm not very good company, I guess."

"I'm much the same," she told him.

"Oh!" Gordon lurched to his feet. "Sorry! My manners—please forgive. Sitting here, leaving a lady standing. Let me find you a chair."

"To tell you the truth, that would be great. I'm not used to wearing grown-up-lady shoes and my feet are killing me. They're also freezing."

Gordon produced a straight chair from farther back under the haymow and pulled it forward for her.

"Evidently, they didn't insulate this old barn when they renovated. I was sitting here thinking that the oil bill must be socking! Charming though. *Drips* with goddam charm," said Gordon sarcastically.

Side by side, they watched Deke perform with the pilot fish. His arm shot in the air as he raised a toast to somebody or something, and his acolytes quickly did the same.

"Have you known Deke long?" Nell asked casually.

"Not really. Helene came across him when she was prowling around for 'Good Works'. Came up with this Children of Woe thing."

"What's your impression of him?" Nell aimed for an off-hand tone.

"Kernow? He's a bit full of himself, I'd say."

Gordon paused for a sip of something dark. Nell wondered how he'd avoided the pale bubbly.

"Sort of a Gatsby character though," Gordon continued musingly. "There's something phony about him."

Nell was instantly alert. "Oh? How do you mean?"

"Can't say, really. It's just a smell." Gordon shot his cuff and peeked at his watch. "I've been around the block a long time, and I can smell a phony. Can smell 'em every time. I think I'll go and try to pry Helene out of her enchantment. Enough is enough."

He stood.

"I've enjoyed talking to you though. Everybody talks like machine guns at these bun fights, but few people say anything worthwhile at all."

Nell stood too.

"I'm right on your heels," she told him. "If I can ever find my coat, that is."

She was in her car and coaxing the heater into full throttle when she realized she hadn't seen the Third Mrs. Kernow. Nell was disappointed. She'd wanted to see those $745 shoes.

～

Chapter 18

It took three calls to Patty Morrissey before a meeting with Ira Zayder, the fund's elusive attorney and financial maven, was achieved. But here at last was Nell, climbing the worn stairs to the headquarters of The Children of Woe Fund. Opening the door and stepping into the harbor view was only slightly less amazing than the first time she'd seen it. Today, rain slanted into the water. Harbor, rocks, rain and the roiling clouds above were all shades and tones of gray and together contrived spread a scene of drama before her. Nell paused to absorb the view before turning to the office.

Once again, it was the sense of Patty Morrissey's eyes on her that drew Nell back to place and time. She recovered quickly.

"Good Morning."

Miss Dry Ice inclined her head in acknowledgement then spoke over her right shoulder.

"Mr. Zayder, Mrs. Bane is here to see you."

Nell followed the direction of Patty's address and realized there was a man seated at a desk in the office's darkest corner. Here was this magnificent view and he'd chosen to live like a bat in the single cave-like space this office afforded. She stepped toward him, offering her hand as she went.

"Please call me Nell. I've really been looking forward to meeting you."

Zayder didn't look up.

Nonplused, Nell slowly dropped her hand to her side and waited. Ira Zayder appeared engrossed in a page of figures. He realized she was standing there, Nell was sure of that, so he was pretending. She observed that his eyes were not moving, and she formed the opinion that he was rude. She stared at the top of his head. Dark hairs encircled a bald spot creating a tonsure. *Long dark hairs.* Nell took some satisfaction in inspecting this. It probably wasn't Zayder's best feature, and Nell hoped he'd have been mortified to have it so prominently available for view. The bald area featured several large freckles. Nell counted them. Seven.

Zayder finally caved to the pressure of the silence and her boring gaze and looked up, annoyed at the interruption. Having introduced herself once, Nell was damned if she'd do it again.

"You probably know that David Kernow has contracted me to write his story," she said. "The story of The Children of Woe Fund, actually. And he tells me you were instrumental in setting up the fund and are active in overseeing its business. I am very interested in hearing what you can tell me about this."

This opening was met with silence; then Zayder gave a grudging grunt and gestured toward a straight chair beside his desk.

"Siddown. I don't know what I can tell you that Mr. Kernow can't or hasn't."

"Well, to start, you could tell me what *you* do for Children of Woe."

The request was met with an exaggerated sigh.

"I handle the funds that come in, okay? I have established an endowment and this requires meticulous oversight, and I must invest the funds judiciously so that monies can be paid out to deserving individuals and families."

"Just for victims of 9/11?"

"Originally that was the case, certainly, but over time, the needs of those children and families have decreased. Kids grew up. College—a lot of them went through college and are now on their own—working—and if I may say, we are proud to have lessened the burdens of student loans on these individuals. Anyhow, now we have expanded and are positioned to help victims of all sorts of terror. I am very sorry to say, there is no shortage of those victims."

"How do you raise your money?"

"That's Mr. Kernow's area. I don't get involved. Ask him."

Ira Zayder's eyes returned to his figures as if pulled there. Nell felt his attention slipping away.

"What else do you do, Mr. Zayder?"

"What?"

"Are you otherwise employed? I understand you're an attorney, do you practice somewhere?"

Ira Zayder seemed distinctly uncomfortable with the question, in fact he appeared disturbed by the direction the conversation seemed to be taking.

"Yes," he said curtly, "but those are not matters germane to this discussion. And as a matter of fact, I have pressing work right now, so if we're finished here, Mrs.? Miss?"

"Nell Bane. And I guess we are."

Nell placed her card on his desk. "I'd appreciate speaking with you further if you..."

But Ira Zayder was already pretending to be engrossed in his figures, and he waved her comment away impatiently. Nell continued to sit for a few moments, but when Zayder didn't look up, she gathered her things. Ira Zayder did not stand up when she did. On her way to the door, Patty Morrissey caught her eye almost apologetically. Surprised, Nell shrugged and gave her a weak smile.

∽

Chapter 19

Nell was trying to figure where she was with Deke Kernow's project at this point and where she needed to go from here. When she had gathered all the information she needed, she would declare herself close to two-thirds of the way to the project's end. Then she would be ready to put her laptop on the kitchen counter and write in earnest, aiming to produce the first draft of the manuscript

"Okay," she said out loud. "This is what I know:

I know that David Kernow is a good-looking, hale-fellow-well-met, back-slapping guy.

I know that, except for his relationship with his grandmother, his childhood was not warm, and I figure that early experiences like that always have an effect on later life—especially when a father is as cold and tough as Deke's father apparently was. In Deke's case, however, I don't yet, understand what that effect could be.

I know he graduated from MIT, therefore, he is intelligent and has a solid technical background.

I figure he must be very well connected socially in Boston and New York circles because he has been successful at putting the bite on people for venture capital for his start-ups and for charitable donations to The Children of War Fund.

Because of the experience with Rose Soon, I know he is capable of deep feeling for human suffering—even to the extent of chucking over his career and company to found the Fund.

I know that he has witnessed a great horror—a tremendous, unspeakable horror—a life-changing event that has, in fact, changed his life.

I know he cheated death literally by minutes.

I know he is grateful for his narrow escape—grateful enough to put his life on a new road.

I know he believes his story is so powerful and dramatic that he wants it told in book and a movie. And I understand that this kind of desire has to be powered by a very strong ego.

I know he has been married three times and that he doesn't talk much about his wives, including the present one, and I know he has had no children.

I know he is capable of decidedly callous treatment toward his administrative assistant, Patty Morrissey. In fact, he treats Patty and the Third Mrs. Kernow—the 3MK—more like possessions than people. And furthermore, I know that his attitudes and treatment of Patty and the 3MK are not in consonance with his treatment of Rose Soon. This is puzzling.

I know the names of his former business partners, and I also know the name of his roommate at MIT; this is useful because I can tap any of these people for information that may flesh out Deke's book.

I know that I don't like his attorney, Ira Zayder, but apart from Zayder's abnormally bad manners, I don't know why I dislike him.

I know that Gordon Porter, among certain others apparently, regards him as a latter-day Gatsby—in other words, a high-flying, exhibitionistic phony. Could this view possibly have merit?

I know he likes mid-century art and design.

"Now with all that I know," Nell continued, "what more do I need to know? What do I have to find out? Where are the clues?

The connections? And what are the outliers? How does this story fit together, and why am I having trouble seeing the whole picture?"

She re-read her inventory, trying to find connections, looking for unusual bits that mightn't figure seamlessly into the whole picture. Where were the outliers?

"Why," she asked herself, "could he be so tender with a Rose Soon and so cavalier with the feelings of a Patty Morrissey and even of a wife?"

"Why," she continued, "did Deke seem so easily bored with businesses he had started? Was he a dilettante—merely a feckless dabbler in the arts and other ventures?"

"How," she muttered, "could he work with a rodent like that nasty Ira Zayder?"

By the end of the exercise, Nell had more questions and no answers. In fact, she felt like she had been swimming a long distance in very muddy water. She shook her head to clear it, but in the end, decided to simply muddy things further by having a glass of wine. And while she sipped it, she concocted a pot of soup for supper.

NELL'S CAULIFLOWER SOUP

1 medium leek, cut into half-inch slices
1 teaspoon of butter
1 tablespoonful of water
1 two-pound cauliflower cut into one-inch pieces
2/3 teaspoon of coriander
1-3/4 cups chicken broth
1-1/4 cups 1% milk
1 teaspoon of black pepper

Nell washed the leeks, dried them carefully, and sliced them up. She melted the butter with the water in a pan, then stirred the leeks and cauliflower until they began to soften. In went the coriander, then the broth and milk and Nell slowly cooked this until the vegetables were very tender. After nearly a half hour, she judged the soup sufficiently cooked, so pulled out the immersion blender and pureed the mixture. Then she finished her wine.

"Tomorrow morning," Nell told herself as she rinsed the blender, "the locks will have tumbled and connections will have fallen into place. Tomorrow I will find that the puzzle will be solved."

She hoped.

~

Chapter 20

Nell was going to another fund-raiser, this one at the Fairmont Copley—a very elegant affair, she gathered. Robert was going too. Apparently everyone Deke ever knew or had accepted a donation from, had received an invitation. Nell and Robert both qualified. So Nell had written another check to The Children of Woe Fund and sent it off with her acceptance card, and she had dragged out the LBD and Nine West sandals once more. She'd be grateful for Robert's presence. For one thing, he always looked like he could moonlight as a model for Louis of Boston and for another, it was so much easier to go to these affairs with someone riding shotgun. She planned to drive into Boston, then she and Robert would taxi to the Copley.

It had changed, the Copley Plaza. It had been co-opted by the Fairmont outfit, and its somewhat dated luster had been considerably buffed up. But still, Nell was pleased to note, some landmarks of old Boston had been retained. She and Robert passed between the gold lions standing sentry at the Dartmouth Street entrance and moved with the crowd through the blue and gold lobby, to the Oval Room. It was lovelier than Nell remembered, and she marveled that Deke had secured this venue. Had dared to engage a room so outstanding.

"This room must have cost a packet and a half," she murmured to Robert.

Robert was a very satisfactory-looking companion, tall and distinguished in black tie. He had been kind to tell her that she looked especially lovely this evening. He smoothly procured a glass of Champagne for each of them and held his up in silent toast to her.

"Seriously, Robert," she said, "what did this room cost, d'you think?"

"I've never even been close to arranging this sort of function," Robert admitted. "Any guess I'd make would have no absolutely grounding in experience."

"Well, here's what I wonder," Nell continued in that low tone, meant only for Robert's ears. "Will Deke garner enough money this evening to pay for the room and the reception and the booze and still substantially fatten the coffers of The Children of Woe Fund?"

Robert shrugged. "We can only guess, but I have to suppose he can. Otherwise, why would he do it?"

The Oval Room was filling fast. Chamber musicians were arranging themselves in a corner near a harp, and now a woman in a long black gown rippled her fingers along the strings summoning music like falling water. Nell's gaze traveled the room. She recognized several television personalities. The funny thing was about celebrities and personalities, she thought, you didn't identify them immediately. Their identities were like developing prints in a darkroom, coming into slow focus before emerging as recognizable entities. There were a number of people she couldn't identify—also celebrities, she assumed. People known in Boston charitable circles, sports figures, perhaps and politicians most probably. She recognized several faces from the barn event in Lexington. And there, in fact, were Kenny and Diane, the hosts.

She glimpsed Helene Porter making her way purposefully across the floor and figured that if she kept Helene in her sights, she'd soon spot Deke. And she did. She saw him lean to kiss Helene's cheek and watched the silly woman preen. Nell looked around for her party-buddy Gordon but didn't see him. Well, if she skirted the edges of the pretty room, she'd come across him, she figured, settled uncomfortably for the evening in one of the gold bamboo chairs.

Nell and Robert mingled. Robert introduced her to several acquaintances from his publishing circle, and Nell was surprised to run into a selectman from Newburyport and was pleased to be able to introduce him to Robert. They spoke very briefly to Deke, who was busy-busy in the midst of another school of pilot fish, also busy-busy swimming at his sides and in his wake. They nibbled little things on sticks that passed and re-passed. Nell refused the stuffed mushrooms on the grounds that they couldn't be consumed politely; juice always spurted or stuffing spilled down your dress. They examined the buffet offerings that were being ravaged by a horde of very well-dressed and noisy jackals.

"Had enough?" Robert asked.

"I have," Nell responded. "We made our appearance. And made our donation, and that's the point of all this, I gather. I don't know, Robert, I guess I'm just a girl from Newburyport, but I'd rather have put my check in the mail and stayed home in front of the fire, knowing that most of my money was going to help some child who'd seen terrible tragedy. And not," she looked with distaste at a chunky woman who was finally shoving away from the buffet with a heaped plate, "feeding someone who could stand to miss a few meals."

"Now, now. Be charitable."

Robert, with his hand in the small of Nell's back, steered her gently out of the Oval Room. In the lobby, she discovered Gordon Porter seated on one of the crimson damask sofas. He was staring, as he had been in the barn, at nothing at all.

"Hello again," said Nell, pausing before him. "Still waiting for your wife to finish partying, I see."

Startled, Gordon raised his eyes, then smiled—a wonderful smile but a little sad. "It will be a long night," he sighed. "Are you leaving? I envy you."

Nell gave him a little shoulder pat. "The night is still young. I'll look for you at the next fund-raiser."

"I will be there," Gordon said wearily. "After all, I've got to drive the car. And write the checks."

～

Chapter 21

"Deke," Nell had said on the phone, "we are closing in on the information-gathering part of our project—the background stuff I need in order to hunker down and start writing the manuscript. But I need to have just a few more details and perhaps some clarifications. Can we get together for one more session?"

Deke had cleared his calendar for her, and she was back in the study in Lexington. The furniture, now familiar, no longer caused flashbacks to the 'fifties.

"Okay," said Nell. "Some of the things we've talked about in the past couple months are confusing me. I need to gain a little more understanding, so I hope you'll excuse any questions that might seem intrusive."

Deke spread his hands. "I'm an open book," he smiled. "Ask away."

"Well, this is delicate." Nell looked down at her lap. A private person herself, she was uncomfortable prying. "You told me you've been married three times, but you didn't give any details. I'm wondering why that is and whether you want to expand that for your book."

"Nope." Deke said.

Then he grinned.

"Just kidding. First wife—we were both in our twenties. Too young, probably. Catherine Harmon couldn't wait to be married until she found out marriage wasn't what she expected. Wasn't like the novels and the magazine articles. I was working straight out, all hours, on the SemiConsolidated start-up, and Catherine didn't feel there was enough of me or enough time left over for her. We were both disillusioned and we—well, we split. Second wife—Gina Collecchio. Gorgeous girl. Looked like Rita Hayworth and just as hot. But there was a clash of cultures. The gap was too wide. Gina wanted a big house in Lynnfield and trips to the North End every Sunday to spend time with mama. She had five brothers—all named Tony—*brrr!* I'm joking, of course. One was named Joey. Scary!"

Deke pretended to shudder.

"Then there's my present wife, and that's the story."

Nell waited for further elaboration. When it didn't come, she probed.

"Deke." Nell said—she said it slowly and distinctly, "what's her name? We've met, but I don't even know her name."

"June."

Nell waited. She waited some more

"June," she repeated.

"That's correct."

Nell wasn't intrepid enough to prod further. She leaned back in her chair.

"Okay," she continued. "Patty Morrissey, how did you come to hire her for The Children of Woe Fund?"

"Patty is the niece of an associate of mine. She was a little down on her luck, I guess, and I hired her as a favor. She's worked out fine. Shows up on time, does what's required of her. I've no complaints."

"Ira Zayder."

Deke shot a sharp glance at Nell.

"Why do you ask?"

"Just trying to get a bit more insight on some of the players," Nell replied innocently.

"I believe I told you that I'd done some work off and on with Zayder prior to 9/11. He's sharp. And he's experienced in the kind of work necessary for the foundation."

"I didn't get much out of him when I asked about the details of his function at The Children of Woe Fund."

"Ira isn't forthcoming. Well, he set up the charitable stuff, the 501(c)(3). He cut through all the red tape crap that I can't be bothered with. And he invests the monies that come in and manages investments and pays the bills. That's pretty much it."

"So he writes the checks for expenses."

"Right."

"Like that bash at the Copley Plaza."

"Right."

"That must have cost a pretty penny," Nell remarked, fishing.

Deke simply gazed at her.

"How is an event like that justified?"

"You just go to the bottom line," Deke told her. "Did you take in more money than went out the door? If the answer is yes, then everything's fine and dandy."

"And the answer was yes."

Deke nodded firmly.

"I asked Mr. Zayder point-blank how charitable monies are raised. I have observed first hand, quite obviously, that you have a substantial list of donors who are invited to fund-raisers, but I haven't seen evidence of other activities. You must have others."

Deke nodded. "Of course. We have a strong online presence and do a little telephone solicitation as well."

Nell was perplexed. "I didn't see any activity like that either time I visited the offices."

"Ira handles it, and it's handled off-site. He has a nephew who does the website. The kid is probably as charming and extroverted as his Uncle Ira."

"About how much money do you raise, Deke?"

"Oh, four to five million a year, give or take."

"And how much does The Children of Woe Fund distribute each year?"

"Almost all of it. You saw the office, you saw the staff—lean and mean. Very low overhead."

"Do you take a salary? Does Ira?"

"Only very modest ones, my dear. Only very modest ones."

Deke had maintained a wide smile during Nell's questioning, but now she got the feeling that the smile was stretched and that Deke's face was tired of being stretched.

He slapped the table with the palms of both hands.

"Are we done here? Are you satisfied?"

Nell nodded.

"And now I have a couple of questions. How is the information-gathering coming along? Are you about ready to start putting pen to paper in earnest?"

Nell capped her pen and closed her notebook.

"Absolutely, Mr. Kernow, I think we're ready to roll."

～

Chapter 22

"I'm throwing a dinner party, Robert," Nell had said on the phone. "It is a delaying tactic, of course. I'm meant to be working on Deke's book and I'm looking for ways to avoid it. Bring Jerry. Tell him there'll be Yankee Gumbo."

"Yankee gumbo? You couldn't keep him away. We'll both look forward to it."

"I've asked the Fitzmaurices and Bunty Whitney as well, so it will be a very artsy-slash-intellectual evening. You're meant to supply the lit'ry element so brush up on your book reviews."

"Fitzmaurice," Robert mused. "He's the ethics professor, isn't he? From B.U.?"

"That's right."

"And his wife Ann is the portrait painter."

"Correct."

"Just checking," Robert said. "Always good to have the cast of characters straight.

"And you know Bunty, of course, my neighbor."

"Who could forget Bunty! It'll be nice to see her again."

And now the little party was in full swing. Nell, face flushed, happily gave the simmering gumbo a turn with a wooden spoon every time she passed the Aga. It had been ages since she'd given a dinner party and now she couldn't think why she'd let it be so long, for she loved cooking for people, and she loved it when the elderly little house was loud with erupting laughter and footsteps and slamming doors. All day Friday, as she chopped and stirred, she'd scarcely given a thought to Deke Kernow and the Hollywood thriller she was meant to be writing. This welcome hiatus ended abruptly when Franklin Fitzmaurice raised the subject.

"How's the book going, Nell? I understand it's a nail-biter about 9/11. And I hear you're aiming it toward Hollywood."

"Where did you hear that, Franklin?"

"Word gets around. We're all eager to read the latest Nell Bane book. So? What's the report?"

"Most of the background work and research are done, Franklin. Now comes the easy part—just writing it."

Fitzmaurice laughed, but Nell, eager to change the subject on this—her night off from Deke Kernow—asked Ann Fitzmaurice to toss the salad and she set Bunty to slicing bread while she herself began to slide the fish and seafood into the gumbo broth.

"Robert, would you be a love and pour the wine?"

Nell leaned over the pot and tested a mussel. Perfect! She ladled the Yankee gumbo into the big tureen.

"Soups on, everybody!" she called happily. "Forward march to the dining room!"

YANKEE GUMBO FOR A NEWBURYPORT NIGHT

1/2 pound hot sausage such as andouile
1/4 cup vegetable oil
1/4 cup butter
1/3 cup flour
1 large leek, sliced
1 large red bell pepper, chopped
2 ribs of celery, chopped

1 cup of okra
2 cups of chicken stock plus more as needed
2 bottles of clam juice
2 bay leaves
salt and pepper to taste
1/4 teaspoon cayenne pepper
1 large can of stewed tomatoes
1 pound of firm white fish (e.g. cod or haddock), skinned
and cut in bite-sized pieces
Either whole lobster or shrimp
One or more of the following: 2-3 whole lobsters, steamed
plus more lobster meat if desired OR 1 pound of large
shrimp
1 pound mussels
1 pound scallops

Here's what Nell did the day before the party:
She browned the sausage in a Dutch oven. Then she
removed the sausage and used a paper towel to wipe out
the pot. Next, she heated the oil in the Dutch oven and
when it was hot, she swirled in the butter, then stirred in
the flour. She stirred this roux until it was a deep, golden
brown; this took a while—about fifteen minutes, in fact.
Then it was the vegetables' turn. Nell tossed them about
until they were well-coated with the roux, and with a great
deal of sizzling accompanied by a cloud of steam, the
liquids went into the Dutch oven. Nell added tomatoes,
salt, pepper and seasonings and simmered the broth for
a little more than an hour. When it had cooled a bit, she
covered the Dutch oven and slid it into the refrigerator.
This required the rearrangement of a pound of coffee and
a jar of mayonnaise.

On the day of the party, Nell steamed the lobster and

picked the meat, reserving some of the claw shells for "local color". She shelled the shrimp and stripped the veins. She scrubbed the beards of several of the mussels and poked them with the tip of a paring knife to be sure they were lively. Using her favorite butcher knife, she cut the cod into bite-sized pieces. All of these were covered and chilled, ready for their submersion into the gumbo just before serving time.

With the candles aflame and her guests seated, Nell asked a blessing on the table and spoke some words of gratitude. Then she raised her glass of red wine. "To dear friends! Health, happiness, and good cheer."

There was a happy response of "Hear-hears!" and "Good friends!" And then there was silence as spoons dipped into the famous Yankee Gumbo.

Chapter 23

Nell ran her fingers over the keyboard so lightly that no type registered on the screen. Begin. Where? How to write a drama extreme enough for Hollywood? For inspiration, her mind conjured the moody Mystic River then floated the director's name—Clint Eastwood—above the water's murky surface.

Begin. Begin?

Begin at the Trade Center. Open with the drama of the scene—with terror's sounds and smells. Begin with the erupting holocaust. No. Begin moments earlier. Spread out Manhattan's blue September sky and begin rolling the credits upward. Then violate that sky with an explosion that shatters the tranquility and shocks the viewers. Shoot flames and black smoke sideways, then upwards to overtake the sunlight glittering off the still inviolate office window. Windows shatter! Nell shatters them. Causes them to explode. She dives directly into the maelstrom now. Goes bravely into the eye of the storm.

Then...shift to the taxi. A blurred Manhattan swipes past the cab's windows. There's a man in the taxi—a passenger. Nell writes of the urgency of his appointment. He's late. He's nervous. He's pressing the driver to go faster.

"Can't do it, man. Traffic's gridlocked. Can't make this thing fly."

Create the explosion. The flash. There's confusion. Move quickly, quickly! Race now! The taxi stops with a jerk. The driver mutters something unintelligible. The passenger argues: "No, go forward! Keep driving!"

"Can't do it, man. Gotta get outa here!"

"No, no! keep going!"

"Not me, man!"

The taxi starts to turn. The passenger shoves open the taxi door and leaps for the sidewalk. The driver doesn't wait to be paid. With brakes squealing, he finishes a three-point turn and guns away. The man—he's slowly morphing into Deke Kernow—we don't yet know it is Deke—stands stunned on the sidewalk. Now he starts toward the Tower, staggering a bit. Lurching.

Nell has prepared well. She has listened over and over to Deke's recording. She has slowly and painstaking transcribed it. She has written notes and a very rough draft. Now, writing urgently, she doesn't have to check the background—it's all inside her. She's there—there at the Trade Center. There in lower Manhattan on a day when everything is about to change. She's there! Her pulse races as she writes. Her face flushes.

"Hollywood stuff," she mutters, coming up to get a glass of water.

Leaning on the sink, she drinks and stares out the kitchen window. But it isn't the garden, she's seeing, it's lower Manhattan. The brilliant blue sky is obscured with dark, ember-studded smoke. The sky over the Battery won't look blue again for days. For some people, it never will be blue.

She returns to the laptop. The room darkens slowly as the light through the kitchen window blushes with sunset, then fades. Somewhere below her, the boiler kicks on, sending hot water chuntering up through the radiators. Nell doesn't hear the sound. Hasn't felt the room chill nor noticed the house's warming response to the boiler. The backlight from the laptop is her only illumination.

Bent over the keyboard, Nell writes.

~

Chapter 24

"Saw your light on late last night." Bunty Whitney strolled up as Nell was pulling grocery bags out of the car.

"Working," Nell replied wearily. "For three days now I've *lived* in lower Manhattan, trying to get the drama of the Towers to rise up off the page and clutch at the reader's gut."

"Progress?"

"Some. But I can't quite seem to get there." Nell shook her head. "And it's driving me nuts. All I can think to do now is make chicken stock and think some more."

NELL'S STANDARD CHICKEN STOCK

3 carrots, cut into thirds
2 stalks of celery, cut into thirds
1 bulb of fennel, cut into large chunks
3 tablespoons of fennel seeds, toasted
1 teaspoon whole black peppercorns
1 whole chicken, 4 to 6 pounds
2 pounds chicken wings, necks and backs
3 quarts low sodium chicken broth
2 quarts cold water

Nell flung the entire list of ingredients into her stockpot and clapped on the lid. Then, when the mixture reached the boil, she reduced the heat and let the soup simmer, uncovered, for an hour. From time to time she checked to be sure the liquid was barely bubbling and skimmed the surface when foam, looking dirty as brook water, collected at the edges of the pot.

An hour into the process, Nell fished out the whole chicken and dumped it in a large bowl to cool. When there was no danger of burned fingers, she pulled the meat from the bones and put it aside for another day. Back into the pot went the bones. Nell placed a smaller pot lid inside the stockpot to keep the bones submerged, then returned the stockpot to the Aga to simmer for four more hours. The little house took on the fragrance of simmering chicken soup.

Nell prepared an ice bath in a dishpan. She strained the stock through a fine sieve into a large, heat-proof bowl which she floated in the ice bath. She stirred the stock often as it came to room temperature. Ah, at last. Nell ladled the stock into stackable freezer containers, and surveyed her finished work with satisfaction. To seal in the flavors, she'd left a layer of chicken fat on the top of each container, all neatly capped and stored.

"And now I know," she said aloud. "what I need to do tomorrow."

~

Chapter 25

Nell called in a favor from a friend who worked in Admissions at MIT, and the friend, in turn, called someone in the Alumni office and within two hours, Nell had John Altman's phone number in New York City. She'd checked back through her notes to find the name of Deke's freshman year roommate—the fellow he'd stayed with in Manhattan on those fateful days in September 2001. The touchy part now was calling Altman and getting him to speak with her. But in the end, this proved easy. Nothing touchy about it at all. In fact, John Altman seemed pleased to talk—even eager to do so.

With introductions and explanations out of the way—("I'm Nell Bane...ghost-writing a book for David Kernow...story of 9/11.")—Nell opened her interview.

"As I understand it, Deke was staying with you and your wife during the 9/11 events."

"Ah," said John Altman. "Well, that's not exactly accurate. Deke was staying with my *wife*. I was in Italy on business and didn't even know he was there. I'd been in Florence for a week when the Towers were hit, and then it was another whole week before it was possible to get a flight home."

Nell was thunder-struck.

"But Deke said—he specifically *said*—he was with you. Even talked about things you did together. Things you said to each other."

Altman laughed. "Yeah, that sounds like Deke. Listen, he was shacked up with my wife the whole time. *Former* wife. After I finally got home, the whole story came spilling out, and it pretty much busted up the marriage. The marriage was probably doomed in the long run anyway, but Deke helped things along considerably."

The interview wasn't going the way Nell had envisioned, and she cast about now for where her questioning should go next.

"Deke didn't know you were out of town?" Nell asked weakly.

"Oh, he knew." Altman laughed again. "Kellie—that was my wife, Kellie Winterspring, Kellie Smith actually. She changed her name. She wanted to be an actress and had gotten a small part in an off-Broadway thing—God knows how! She had no more talent than a goat but she was good-looking. I'll give her that. Anyway, she and Deke set things up. An assignation, I believe it's called. Apparently Deke drove down on Sunday or Monday and moved in."

"Yes," Nell prompted. "He had a business meeting Tuesday morning in the North Tower. He was late and there was traffic and he got to the Trade Center just in time to see the first plane hit."

Altman snorted.

"Deke Kernow was nowhere near the Trade Center on 9/11! He was safe in bed—in *my* bed—on the upper east side with *my* wife, watching the whole show on television!"

Nell couldn't believe this. Altman was probably bitter—and he had a right to be—but to slander his friend this way was...well, Nell was shocked.

John Altman seemed to have recovered from any bitterness though. In fact, he sounded quite cheerful, and since he seemed in no hurry to conclude the conversation, Nell asked him another question.

"You go quite a ways back with Deke, I believe. Since I'm trying to collect some background information about him, would you mind answering a few more questions?"

"If I can, I'd be happy to help you."

"Thank you. So you and Deke were roommates at MIT?"

"That's right. Freshman year. And what a year that was! Great times. But it almost cost me my scholarship. My parents finally kicked me in the ass. Gave me an ultimatum. Find a new roommate for sophomore year or transfer to UMass. So I finished up freshman year by the skin of my teeth, found a quiet guy from Iowa to share quarters in the fall, then sailed through my sophomore year and straight on through to graduation. Deke lasted six weeks and was gone before Thanksgiving."

Nell, tapping her pen against her check, was trying to work this out.

"So he never graduated?"

"Not from MIT. If he graduated from anyplace, it was probably North Shore Community College."

"Huh. I saw the Brass Rat and figured him for a fond alumnus."

"Aw, he probably picked the ring up on a sink in a men's room. Or bought it on eBay."

"Did you two part brass rags after freshman year?"

"No, we kept in touch off and on, especially after graduation when we were no longer a danger to each other. Or so I thought. I thought he was a great guy. I enjoyed his company. Up to a point."

"What can you tell me about him? About his family maybe? Did you know his father?"

"Well, there was some family money—a trust fund from a doting grandmother—but his father was really disgusted with him and cut him off in the middle of that riotous freshman year. I met old Douglas Kernow once. Once was enough."

"I heard he was pretty cold-hearted," Nell commented.

"To put it mildly! Well. When Deke turned eighteen, which, by the way was shortly after we got on campus, this trust fund from his grandmother kicked in. Deke chewed into Granny's money like a homeless man at a hot lunch. Spent like a sailor on shore leave. That was when his father cut him off for good."

"Yes," said Nell, "he spoke about the car he bought."

"It's a wonder he didn't total it," Altman remarked. "Deke had a habit, common to some wealthy people, of never carrying much cash and sponging off friends and failing to pay them back. Some of us guys were always digging into our pockets at the gas pump. Everything you had was Deke's." The note of bitterness had come back. "But you got very little back from him."

Nell shook her head.

"I can't get over this thing about New York," she said. "He was so convincing. So specific. He talked about your apartment on East 89th."

Nell checked her notes.

"He said that the three of you went to the York Grille on Monday night. You walked there. Then you and he stayed up late talking about old times and sharing a bottle of Scotch."

"Nope," said Altman. "No me. Kellie maybe. But I was in Florence."

Nell couldn't seem to let this go.

"He said he was on Liberty Street approaching Cortland when the North Tower was hit. He described the scene in detail and said he tried to save a young woman named Rose Soon. He said he didn't get back to your apartment until late at night. Claimed you and Kellie had figured he was dead."

"Let me tell you what Kellie said."

There was a steely tone in John Altman's voice now.

"When the Towers were hit, Deke was watching television—*The Today Show*, as a matter of fact. He saw the whole drama unfold from the bed. *Our* bed. He was drinking coffee and Kellie'd probably brought him a bagel with a schmear. He was nowhere near the financial district. The whole story is a fabrication. A figment of his mind. But I can tell you this though—Deke always finds a way to use things to his advantage. He trades on that MIT ring you noticed. He uses it to wheedle funds out of venture capitalists. Convinces them he's technically savvy. He's partnered three start-up companies, all of which foundered and went under. But Deke himself has always trotted off as bright-eyed and bushy-tailed as Bre'r Rabbit hopping out of that briar patch."

"Oh my," said Nell. And then she added, "Oh dear."

Chapter 26

Nell was stunned. She felt like she'd been punched. She could hardly believe these things about Deke. Over the last three months, she'd gotten to know him pretty well. Thought she had, anyway. But John Altman's story had shaken her to her shoes.

Then she began doubting Altman. Could she trust him? Maybe he had an axe to grind and was using it to chop down Deke's character. If Deke did have an affair with this Kellie Winterspring, then Altman probably had a reason to be sore. Maybe angle for revenge. A thousand possibilities spun and tossed and tumbled in Nell's mind like laundry in a clothes dryer. Here the red shirt of scandal, there the blue sock of another point of view.

"I've been a ghostwriter for three decades," she mumbled, "but I've never had to sort out anything like this!"

But once you know something, you can't unknow it, and so Nell, feeling like Pandora, dug deeper into this thing. She didn't like what she was doing, and she didn't like herself for doing it, but she combed through her notes to find the names of Deke's former business partners. If she could get positive character references from them, perhaps that could cancel out Altman's shocking tale—expose it as a lie fabricated for whatever devious reason.

SemiConsoliated had gone out of business. Well, that seemed to jibe with Altman's claim that anything that Deke touched had gone under. Nell couldn't find even a ghost of it on the web. But businesses shift and merge, she knew that, and perhaps SemiConsoliated had been sold to some other outfit. Perhaps its name had been changed.

She did a search for Charlie Carney and got no further. Charlie Carney had disappeared without leaving a slick.

Kernow's parting with his second partner, Jules Stutzman, had been unpleasant. Even if she could find Stutzman, Nell doubted that she could trust anything he might have to say. So that left Bennett and Craddock, who had ventured into the dot-com game with Deke Kernow.

She had no better luck finding CompuSavvy.com than she'd had finding SemiConsolidated. Craig Craddock, however, did turn up in a Google search, and Nell reached him on the telephone. Once again she ran her spiel, and Craddock agreed to meet her for coffee at a Dunkin Donuts near his present operation in Cummings Park.

"So Deke is writing a book, eh?" Craddock helped himself to a laugh. "So how does that work? Does he actually sit down and *write* it?"

"You seem a little dubious about that possibility," Nell told him, a bit tartly.

Craddock laughed again.

"Dubious? You bet! Deke Kernow couldn't keep his attention on anything long enough to write a book. Come on, what's the deal?"

Nell decided she didn't particularly care for this man, but she did need information from him.

"I am a professional ghostwriter," she said. "My clients tell me their personal stories, I record and transcribe those stories, and produce successive drafts that we edit and revise together until we have a book manuscript that the client likes."

"Interesting." Craddock appeared to be thinking. "So what can I tell you?"

"I'd like to know how you met Deke, and how you started up your business. I'm interested in what Deke did in the business, and why you went your separate ways."

"Whew. That's more than one cup of coffee's worth. I may need a donut too."

Nell spread her hands generously. "It's on me. Tell."

"I knew Deke from MIT..."

"Did you graduate together?" Nell asked hopefully.

Craddock looked confused. "Well, no," he said, "We didn't, as a matter of fact. Let's see...we hung out a lot freshman year..." he chuckled reminiscently. "Ya see, Deke had this car..."

"He looked across at Nell who was waving away this story which she'd heard once from Deke and again from Altman.

"Well, okay, we knew each other from freshman year, and after that I'd see Deke around campus from time to time. He dropped out for a while, and I think he transferred someplace else, but I'd see him around Cambridge. Jake Wirth's, the Harvest, the coffee houses. He was always good for a drink and a few laughs. God! Deke Kernow knew everybody."

Nell nodded.

"Your company?" she said encouragingly.

"I got to fooling around—me and this other guy Bennett, Chuck Bennett—with a technology called computer signal processing and some other computational technologies that crunch enormous numbers at fantastic speeds and requiring, by the way, smaller and smaller chasses to do the job. Bennett was older than I. He'd been working for DEC and a couple other 128 hot tickets, but the dot-coms were just beginning to take off, and we decided to get together and get in on the action. And we did.

We got in soon enough to catch an early flight."

Craddock looked pleased with the figure of speech he'd created.

"So Deke wasn't part of the original arrangement?" Nell ventured. .

"No. We'd already staked out the business plan. We knew where we wanted to go, it was just a matter of getting there."

"And?"

"Well, we needed capital. And more than just a shot from someone's bank account. We needed *venture* capital, but neither Bennett nor I had the time or the connections to get it. That's when I thought of Deke."

"Aha."

"Aha, indeed. I looked up Deke. It wasn't hard to find him. I just trolled through Cambridge and, my god, there he was on a stool at the Harvest!"

This seemed to Craddock to be an uproarious coincidence. Nell waited patiently while his laughter ran down to a trickle and stopped.

"As it happened, Deke was casting about for something new. He'd just walked out of a business thing, and—"

"Yes, can you tell me anything about that?"

"The stuff he'd been doing?"

Nell nodded.

Craddock ran his hand over his chin. "Gosh, I think it was something to do with light. Yeah! LEDs, that was it."

"What do you know about it?"

Craddock shook his head.

"Nope. Sorry. I don't remember anything about it. Come to think of it, I didn't know much at the time. We were focused on CompuSavvy. Didn't much care about history, recent or ancient."

"Okay," said Nell. "Please go on."

"Well, I convinced Bennett that Deke could be the face of the firm. You know? Get out there. Hang face. Cozy up to the deep pockets. And there were some very deep pockets out there then. Everyone with cash in their jeans was hot to get into dot-coms—especially the high tech outfits. So Deke bought into the action. A large influx of cash and—*poof!*—he's a stockholder and minority owner."

"And he wasn't involved in the technology? None of the fast math stuff? I mean, you weren't interested in using any of his technical know-how to develop the product or anything?"

"Technical know-how? You're kidding, right? This is Deke Kernow. He's Charm Boy, not some geek. No. Deke pretty much stayed clear of the day-to-day operation—the technical stuff, the business stuff. He did his work on the road and in restaurants and bars. He schmoozed, he hondled, he tap-danced and sang and made promises. He worked over the financial guys. Convinced them that CompuSavvy was hotter than Digital Equipment. Remember, these were the days when Apple was a pip-squeak company that only graphic artists were enthusiastic about. Bill Gates was just a Harvard drop-out and a lot of guys still thought if you weren't using DOS, you weren't really working."

"Did Deke bring in a lot of...um...dough?"

"He did. But in those days, you gotta remember, people had more money than sense, and they couldn't find enough walls to throw it at."

Craddock chuckled reminiscently.

"Ah, those were the days."

"Was CompuSavvy successful?" Nell asked, being discretely cagey.

"Yeah. Yeah, it was. We went public and the stock hit $98 a share. Deke walked into the office with a case of Dom Perignon. I'll always remember that. Then shit hit the fan."

"I understand Deke left the company in 2001. Right after 9/11. Is that right?

Craddock looked surprised.

"No," he said slowly, "that's not when we parted company with Deke. He left in late 2000. Left when the bubble popped. The stock was down in the dumper. We were eating beans and our own fingernails. There wasn't a cent of venture capital to be scrounged out there. The money wells simply dried up. And Deke's contribution to the company had outlived its value."

Once again Nell was caught flat-footed.

"I thought he'd had some CompuSavvy business in New York. That he'd traveled there the day before 9/11."

Craddock looked blank. Then he shook his head uncomprehendingly.

Nell changed the subject.

"Have you been in touch with Deke? I mean lately?"

"We haven't exactly kept in touch." Craddock's answer was laconic. "Bennett and I had our noses to the grindstone after the bubble. We didn't have the time or interest to follow the further adventures of Deke Kernow. I did run into him a year or so ago coming out of Jake Wirth's. Same old Deke. Big smile, a punch on the shoulder, a big-soul grabbing handshake. I told him he looked great. He did! He asked how the company was doing—great, great. I asked him what he was up to. I remember he said something about a charitable foundation, but we didn't go into it. I wasn't that interested, if you want to know the truth."

Nell was silent, the victim, once again, of a massive information dump. All of this would require sorting out.

"Oh!" she cried, "Gosh! I'm sorry. I promised you a donut, didn't I? And you've finished your coffee."

She started to jump up, but Craddock put a hand on her forearm. "That's okay. I gotta get back. Tell you what—instead of that donut, just send me a copy of the book when it's published. That's a story I'd love to read!"

The molded plastic chair scraped along the floor as Craddock pushed back from the table.

"You've got a deal," Nell told him. But she continued to sit at the round table inside the Dunkin Donuts after Craig Craddock left the shop.

～

Chapter 27

Nell wrote. Even after her meeting with Craig Craddock, she wrote. Couldn't think what else to do. And she had a contract. A deal. And her own ethical code kept her on the job. She wrote all day and all the next day. She wrote into the night. Her printer spit out page after page, then complained of a lack of ink. Nell changed the cartridge. She wrote even later into the night. She summoned her notes and transcripts and recordings. Then ripped open a new ream of paper. She wrote more of 9/11 and of the trip home from New York. Then she began the backstories. She wrote of Hamilton, Massachusetts and the big house off Bay Road. She wrote of Deke's mother and of his stepmother, of his cold father and of his beloved Myrtle Mapes Kernow. She wrote of MIT, and there she stopped.

"I'll come back to this," she murmured.

She went on to write of SemiConsolidated and Charlie Carney, of Jules Stutzman and Kernow Light. She wrote of CompuSavvy and of brash Craig Craddock. But all this was backstory—flashback from 9/11, the heart of Deke's story.

She read what she'd written. Yes. The opening had drama. It had tension. And Nell felt it would bring the desired gut-cramping responses from the readers. Was it Hollywood stuff? Nell couldn't say. She wasn't sure—had never been sure—that Deke's story had the power and appeal of his vision. All she could do was do her best.

She was into The Children of Woe Fund when she hit the next wall. Nell pushed away from the laptop. She needed real people here—real stories that would make this material spark. She thought of the photographs on the walls of Deke's study. Remembering the photo of Deke holding the child, Nell had an *ah-ha* moment. Rose Soon's kids!

What if she were able to find Rose Soon's kids? Yes! The ones who had started this whole adventure.

Google again. This time Nell was searching for Rose Soon—anything about Rose Soon. Basically, a dry socket. She learned that a rare blue rose, soon to be introduced, was causing a great stir among rose enthusiasts, but she did not—*could* not—find a Rose Soon, late of New York City. Or of Brooklyn or Queens or Staten Island.

Without much hope, Nell brought up the complete list of 9/11 victims. She was shaken once again by the awful length of the list. She scrolled down and down to the S's. There was no Soon. Not a Soon of any description—not even an Albert or a Margaret or a Mei. There must be a mistake! Thinking the name may have been mis-alphabetized, Nell read the entire roster of S's. There was a Solomon. A Song. A Soto. There was not a Soon. Had Rose Soon never existed? Was she—Nell—in some kind of Twilight Zone? Nell began to doubt where she was and what she was doing. Her heart was beating faster than it should.

～

Chapter 28

"Robert, I need a reality check."

"Why? What's up?"

"Too complicated to explain on the phone. Also I have to get out of this house because I think I may be going crazy."

"How about meeting me for lunch at the Black Cow?" Robert said. "Before you go crazy, I mean."

"What? Now?"

"I can take a break," Robert said, "and be there in an hour."

"Oh, Robert, you don't know how comforting it is just to hear your voice. I'll go early and snag the booth that feels like a ship's cabin. Then we can look out the window at the river and imagine we're sailing away to somewhere warm and pleasant where they serve pineapple drinks all day long."

So Nell, with her elbow on the table and her chin on her fist, was moodily watching the Merrimac River's capricious current when Robert slid into the booth across from her.

"You look troubled," he said.

"Troubled," she repeated. "That's almost as bad as hearing someone say you look tired. Both, in my opinion, simply mean that you're looking old."

Robert just smiled. And Nell decided to forgive him.

"Okay," she said, "here's the story. I've been learning, in dribs and drabs, that many of the things Deke Kernow has said about himself—some of the claims he's made—aren't exactly, one-hundred percent true."

"You mean he's prone to exaggeration?" Robert asked.

"Yes, that. But that's mild—that's forgivable to some degree. But some of his claims seem to be out-and-out lies."

Robert's eyebrows ascended above his glasses, but typically, he kept silent, allowing her to tell her tale.

"For instance, I had a long conversation with the fellow he was supposed to be visiting in New York on 9/11."

"Yes?"

"The guy was in Italy on business. He wasn't even *in* New York! That was so astonishing—so hard to get my head around—that I blamed the *guy*. His name is John Altman, and I blamed *him!* I thought he must be mistaken! And then, Robert—do you remember this? Do you remember that first time you took me to Deke's house to meet him, and I told you afterward that I thought something was funny? Well, odd? Like he told us he was visiting this friend in New York, and then he talked about a hotel—do you remember I said that was curious? That I remarked on it?"

Robert scratched his jaw. "Yeah, I guess I remember you said something like that."

"Well," Nell hurried on, "this guy—this John Altman—claimed that Deke was shacked up with his wife. *Altman's* wife. And that Deke was nowhere near the Trade Center that morning. That he'd just gone to New York to carry on a tryst with Mrs. Altman, or rather Ms. Winterspring. That's her name—Kellie Winterspring."

Robert was shaking his head. "Wait a minute. Slow down. I'm getting confused."

"I shouldn't wonder," Nell snapped. "It is confusing and it's growing weirder every time I turn around. So I had just about convinced myself that Altman was looking for a way to besmirch Deke, but now I'm not so sure. I started asking around. Snooping. And now I'm coming up with other facts that aren't—well—what they're supposed to be."

"Like?"

"Like Rose Soon. The woman Deke is supposed to have found after the North Tower crashed. The woman he supposedly picked up and carried to some EMT station. The woman who allegedly inspired The Children of Woe Fund. Robert, she doesn't exist."

"Of course, she doesn't," Robert said practically. "She died on 9/11, didn't she?"

"No, I mean she didn't *exist*. She never existed. Deke Kernow made her up. Invented her."

"You're sure?"

"As sure as I can be. I started with the official list of 9/11 victims. Then I searched Social Security records, reverse phone look-ups, everything I could think of. And Robert, believe me, there is not—nor was—any person in New York named Rose Soon."

Nell's non-stop monologue had run down. She sat exhausted and silent. Across from her, Robert was silent as well.

"What are you going to do?" he asked her.

Nell thought. Now that she had opened up her doubts and shared them, she felt strangely calm.

"Deke Kernow is about to pay me the agreed-upon two-thirds of the book I contracted to ghostwrite for him. As I see it, I have a contractual obligation to continue. To finish. So I will finish the first draft and I will deliver it to Deke and go over it with him. There will be changes and revisions and all that stuff. That's to be expected. And I will handle it all. I will see that he gets the manuscript he paid for. But I will do something else too—and this may simply be for my satisfaction—I am going to get to the bottom of this thing. I'm going to find out what is really going on here."

Robert regarded her soberly. "Be careful."

"Oh my, that sounds ominous."

Robert's gaze didn't waver as he repeated his words. "Just be careful."

~

Chapter 29

Gloucester's Inner Harbor was as tranquil as a public swimming pool. The air was soft, the wind was light, the water glittered. Maybe this had a salubrious affect on Patty Morrissey, because she actually thawed a bit when Nell pushed through the door of The Children of Woe offices.

"I'm here to ask favors." Nell stood with both hands up to show she was unarmed and vulnerable, and Patty Morrissey actually almost smiled. Feeling victorious, Nell advanced. "I'm wondering if I might have a peek at the list of people who've donated to The Children of Woe Fund."

By this time, Patty Morrissey had accepted Nell's position in regard to Deke Kernow and The Children of Woe Fund. Nell's credentials were in order. She had achieved clearance.

Patty opened a drawer, withdrew a folder and handed it over without comment.

"I'll just sit over here, shall I?" Nell indicated an empty desk in front of the super window, and indirectly asked Patty's permission.

"Sure. Suits me," Patty said noncommittally, "if it suits you."

And so Nell settled into an upholstered desk chair that could spin toward the harbor view and began to read through the lists of names of those who had written checks—many of them enormously generous—to Deke's charity. She recognized a number of names—not because she knew the donors personally, but because they were names of note in and around Boston. The towns of Weston and Dover were well represented. Brookline and Cambridge, as would be expected, showed up frequently. Then Nell came upon someone she knew. Well, sort of knew. Gordon and Helene Porter listed as significant contributors to The Children of Woe Fund.

"I wonder..." Nell murmured. She stared out of the harbor without really seeing it, lost in thought.

Then she quickly wrote down the Porters' address and phone numbers. One number matched the Weston exchange, but the other was a Boston number. Figuring this to be Gordon's office, Nell underlined the second number. It was Gordon to whom she wanted to speak. Helene, for Nell's purposes, would be useless.

"All set?" Patty Morrissey asked as Nell rose from the borrowed desk.

"I think so. For now anyway. But, Patty, I wonder if I might ask you a question or two—you wouldn't have to answer if you feel it's intrusive."

In response, Patty folded her hands with little girl precision and leaned forward on the desk. Nell took this listening posture as an affirmative.

"You've been working for The Children of Woe for sometime, I gather."

Patty nodded. "From the beginning, just about."

"And you've certainly seen it grow, become more successful."

Patty nodded again.

Nell plunged ahead. "What's your take on Deke?"

Now Patty unfolded her hands and leaned back in her chair,

withdrawing her forthcoming posture.

"He's my boss—obviously—and I don't know how much I'm at liberty to say."

"I wouldn't want you to compromise yourself," Nell said hastily. "I was just wondering, that's all. I'm asking around, getting different perspectives on who Deke Kernow is. Thought I'd give you a chance to speak your piece, and one thing I've noticed—and this has puzzled me—is the way he sometimes treats you."

Nell watched Patty carefully. "He can be a very gracious man," she continued. "Charming even, but he orders you around and sometimes he's almost rude."

"Yeah—well, you got that right! Sometimes he treats me like a piece of furniture. Oh, sometimes he's okay but then something crawls up his dress and he starts unloading a ton of crap on me—yelling, asking me if I'm stupid."

Nell's eyebrows shot up.

"There are times when I simply hate him, and then other times—well, other times, he's okay."

Patty's face had reddened. She dropped her eyes.

"And I've seen a few things that I haven't much liked around here, I guess. But I need the job, so I try to keep my mouth shut, do my work and mind my own affairs but...well, let me just say there are some business practices around here that aren't the best."

Nell cocked an eyebrow. "Can you give me an example?"

"For instance Mr. Zayder pays all Mr. Kernow's bills. I don't know whether that's kosher or not. Like, should the foundation be picking up Mr. Kernow's mortgage? Should it be paying his medical expenses? I understand, of course, that his travel and entertainment expenses could be legitimately paid, but I'm pretty sure that his wife's membership at the tennis club is a stretch."

Now Patty pushed back in her chair, shaking her head. "There now! I've said too much! You shouldn't have got me started!"

"I get the feeling," Nell said, "that you've been wanting for quite some time to vent about this though."

Patty nodded, looking miserable.

"Well," Nell said consolingly, "we'll keep this just between us. It'll go no farther than this room. This information is outside my sphere of interest anyway. I'm writing a book about Deke's story, not about his bank account or business practices. And Patty—I'm sorry if I've upset you, if this conversation has been uncomfortable. Let's forget it. I know I will."

Patty Morrissey swallowed. "Thank you," she whispered.

Nell, with a smile of reassurance, waved from the door of The Children of Woe Fund office.

~

Chapter 30

Taking a risk, Nell punched up the second phone number she'd copied—the number she figured was Gordon Porter's office—and breathed a relieved sigh when she heard Gordon's voice after the second ring.

"Gordon, this is Nell Bane. I'm going out on the limb here by hoping you'll remember me. We've met twice actually. The first time was at a fund-raiser in Lexington. In a barn. You were kind enough to keep me company under the haymow."

The introduction was rewarded with a chuckle.

"Yes, I do remember you. And I remember that we met again in the Copley Plaza. I preferred the interior decoration in the barn, if you want to know. What can I do for you?"

"I wanted to have a short conversation with you about our mutual acquaintance—David Kernow."

"Ah. Well, I don't know Kernow all that well, but go ahead."

"You and your wife have been contributing to The Children of Woe Fund for quite a while. Are you satisfied with the charity? Do you and she feel that your contributions are providing worthwhile help and support to the survivors of terror?"

"I have no reason to believe that they're not helping," Gordon

Porter said carefully, "but I should make clear that the charity work is mainly of my wife's doing. She believes in the foundation passionately, but between you and me, I think she's far more interested in the foundation's founder than in the distribution of charitable funds."

"And what do *you* think of the foundation's founder, Gordon?"

Nell held her breath.

"I think Deke Kernow is an empty drum—all noise and very little substance."

"If that's the case, Gordon, why do you continue to contribute?"

"My wife. Kernow's is only one of Helene's little causes. She runs from one to another—another party dress, another pair of shoes, hopefully another picture in the *Globe* or *Boston Magazine*. It is a relatively harmless pastime, and right now she's half in love with Kernow—more than half, I'd say. And she's not the only one. You've seen that crowd of groupies that follows him at fund-raisers. Most of them are like Helene—frustrated and discontented wives who need to be reassured that they are desirable. And if they aren't young enough and gorgeous enough to attain it on their own, they try to buy desirability with charitable donations. Kernow knows this. He collects these women. He cultivates them. And flirts with them, then cashes their checks. And what these women get in return, in addition to feeling desired, is the sense that they are doing "great works.""

Nell was stunned by Gordon Porter's frankness.

"And what do *you* get out of it all?"

"I," said Gordon Porter, "get some peace and quiet. When Helene's distracted—when she's chasing another cause, another dress, another social affair—I get to sit quietly in my study, thinking long, long thoughts about anything I care to think about."

"But the money...?"

"We can afford to write the checks. And who knows? Some of

that money may actually end up doing some good."

"I hope it does, Gordon, I sincerely hope it does. And I must tell you I admire you very much indeed and thank you for your honesty."

"Will I see you at the next fund-raiser?" Gordon asked. "Helene tells me there's a helluva wing-ding coming up at some country club. Winchester, I think."

"I hadn't heard about that, and I'd probably give it a miss," Nell told him. "But you will be the very first person I seek out the next time I attend a Children of Woe function."

~

Chapter 31

The Children of Woe Fund website was attractive, understated even, but thin on content, Nell thought. She remembered the mission statement from the letterhead, but Nell, trying to discover what the foundation had actually done, kept running into blank walls. She tried the tab labeled: "Our Donors" where there were categories based on dollar amounts. This, Nell knew, was typical. The Children of Woe categories were headed: "Angels"—a lofty list of foundations and individuals who had given $100,000 and above—followed by "Super Heroes" ($25,000 and more), "Heroes" ($10,000 or more), "Benefactors" ($1,000 or more) and finally, "Friends" ($100 or more). Nell observed there wasn't a category for donations less than $100, and she wondered what such a group might be called, if there were one.

"Pals?" she speculated. "Chums?"

Donations of goods and services were also acknowledged as well as donations made in memory of individuals.

Nell inferred that these donations had not come from fundraisers but almost entirely from online contributions, and she clicked with keen interest on the tab that invited her to "Donate Now."

She read that all donations were welcome, and she learned that all donations were tax deductible to the extent the law allowed. As on the letterhead, she was invited to select one of three colors for the wristband that would be mailed to her in acknowledgement of her contribution.

Nell scrolled to the very bottom of the page and squinted at the 8-point type, rendered in pale gray ink, searching until she found the site's webmaster. The name gave away little. RAZ Enterprises. It took Nell almost half a day to follow the trail that led to RAZ Enterprises, but she traced it, finally, to an address in Watertown, where someone named Richard Zayder ran a web design and management firm.

Bingo.

"Only connect," murmured Nell.

If there was any hanky-panky in the fund management, Nell thought, it would be here with whatever scheme Richard and Ira might be running.

But this was not her mission. It wasn't the puddle she needed to play in.

"I was hired to write Deke Kernow's book," Nell reminded herself sternly. "That's all. Keep your eye on the ball, Eleanor!"

∾

Chapter 32

Now, with the first draft of Deke's book complete, Nell was delivering it to the house in Lexington.

"Phoenix Ascending: Rebirth From The Flames of September 11th, read Deke aloud. He ran his hand reverently over the title page of the draft Nell had brought him—the first, finished draft of his story. He looked up with the bright expression of a little boy at his own birthday party.

"Is this the title you've come up with?" he asked hopefully. "I like it. Yes, I like it! So what's the next step? What happens now?"

"Now," Nell told him, "you read the draft. I suggest you read it straight through, resisting attempts to wield a red pen. Gather your first impressions. See whether the story moves you. Pay attention to your gut. Then read it again with the red pen in hand. Finally, we'll get together and talk about what you like, what you may not like and what changes we need to make in the second draft."

Deke nodded. His hand was still moving across the binder as if he could hardly register the wonder of holding his own book manuscript.

"When do I see the actual book?" he asked.

"What you do with the manuscript is up to you. You can seek a publisher or you can publish it yourself. But I strongly suggest you speak to Robert Hutchins before you do anything. This is his field and he will have sound advice."

"Is there any other business we have to do?" Deke said.

"The business now is on your end." Nell smiled. "Read, my friend. Read and God speed."

She stood to go.

"Wait!" Deke commanded. He jumped up from his chair and hurried to the desk where he scrawled out a check.

"As per our contract," he told her, handing over the check with some ceremony. "Two-thirds of the way through the project earns two-thirds of the money."

Nell folded the check and tucked it into her bag.

"Thank you," she said. "I'll see myself out. You get busy reading."

As she stepped through the study door, she smiled to see Deke's head was already bent over the binder. She pulled the door closed softly and ran right into the Third Mrs. Kernow, scuttling like a mouse along the hall, head down.

"Oh!" cried Nell, startled.

The 3MK looked up sharply, and Nell uttered a second, involuntary cry of exclamation.

"Oh my!"

But the woman—practically running now—sprinted down the hall before Nell got a second look at the blackened eye and the bruised jaw.

~

Chapter 33

For the first time in—what?—Nell couldn't remember how long, but it was weeks anyway, Deke's book project was not hanging over her head, wasn't niggling at her conscience, wasn't scolding her to get to that computer and get busy. Luxury!

She slept in—well, until seven-thirty anyhow. She took long walks. She revisited all the shops on State Street, buying lovely things in her mind. And she made a perfect French onion soup.

Nell had strong opinions about onion soup. First, the onions. She didn't like long, wet strings of onion draggling down your chin when you lifted a spoon to your lips. Halving or even quartering the onions before slicing them was essential. Then there was the matter of a topping. A crouton, yes, but Nell considered the practice of finishing onion soup with a thick crust of broiled cheese to be barbaric at best and at worst, downright dangerous. Her prejudice against draggling onions carried over to draggling cheese which could burn mouths and chins, and she—Nell—had heard of one horrifying instance when someone almost choked to death on a wad of melted cheese and had been saved by an alert chef who leapt in and performed the Heimlich maneuver.

FRENCH ONION SOUP

5-6 six cups of thinly sliced yellow onions, halved or quartered if quite large)
3 tablespoons of butter
1 tablespoon of olive oil
1 teaspoon of salt
1/2 teaspoon of sugar
3 tablespoons of flour
2 quarts of boiling beef stock of excellent quality
1/2 cup of dry white wine—preferably vermouth
1/4 cup brandy or cognac

Nell "melted" the onions by cooking them very slowly in a covered pan for 20 minutes. Then she uncovered the pan and sprinkled them with the salt and sugar—the sugar, she knew, would help the onions caramelize, bringing them to a deep, golden brown. Then, still stirring, she dusted the onions with flour; Nell stirred them for 3 minutes to cook away the raw, floury taste while providing thickening.

She got out a second pan for the stock, which she brought to a boil. Then she pulled the onion pan off the heat and slowly poured the boiling stock over the onions.

When the onion soup had simmered, partially covered, for almost three-quarters of an hour—and when Nell had vigilantly skimmed the broth as needed—she pronounced her soup finished. Finished except for the cognac, which she stirred in just before serving.

As the onions melted, Nell thought about Deke Kernow. She envisioned him reading through the draft of the book, and try as she would, she couldn't evict him from her mind. What might he be thinking as he actually read those lies? Read them on paper in

black and white? Did he believe he was drawing near the Trade
Center on that clear, blue morning the Towers were hit? Had he
convinced himself he smelled the stink of destruction? Found Rose
Soon? Had the path of his life turned 180 degrees and his feet set
on a new path? Did he believe his own publicity? Could he even
tell the difference between truth and the lie?

"Damn!" exclaimed Nell, punctuating her exclamation with a
slammed pot lid, "I'm supposed to be on hiatus! Why can't I put
this down?"

～

Chapter 34

"I need your professional opinion, Bunty," said Nell.

"On pottery? What the hell for?"

"No. Not pottery, on your former profession."

"Oh, crap!" said Bunty. "That! I took up pottery to get out of that psycho racket."

"Bunty!" Nell was shocked. "You didn't talk that way to your clients, I hope."

"Of course not. I was the very model of a modern psychotherapist, but the thing was, Nell, some of those people were unhinged."

"Yes, and you helped many of them. I've heard that. I know something of your reputation. Now. How about getting together for coffee and helping me sort something out."

"Are you paying for my expertise?"

"I'm paying for the coffee. Now have we got a deal?"

Bunty Whitney had given up cigarettes five years earlier, but she still claimed—frequently and loudly—to miss them, and her voice still retained the raw and rusty hoarseness of a confirmed, longtime smoker.

"Okay," she said, "what are you so hot to 'sort out'?"

So Nell spent the next fifteen minutes pouring out to Bunty the story of David Kernow and the bits and pieces that simply didn't add up.

"He's supposed to be this tender-hearted humanitarian," she complained finally, "but then he treats the people closest to him— his wife, his administrative assistant—like slaves. Worse than slaves, he treats them like *objects*. He calls them by titles—'my wife', 'my secretary'. On the one hand, he can be moved to tears by a little girl who lost a parent, and then he turns around and is unspeakably rude to Patty Morrissey. He can apparently change the course of his entire life because he meets—for fifteen minutes—a woman named Rose Soon, and he uses the *idea* of her children—children he's never even met—as the motivation for establishing an entire charitable foundation."

Nell paused for a sip of coffee.

"And I have direct testimony from people who know Deke well—people like John Altman and Craig Craddock who've known him for years—that he's not entirely who he claims to be. And there are other people, Gordon Porter for instance, who regard him simply as a shameless self-promoter. He's there for the parties. He's at the center of attention—and you should see him, Bunty! Swarms of women all around him, yapping and lapping at him like...like lapdogs, and he's eating it up. *And* taking their money!"

Nell ran out of breath.

Bunty listened in absolute silence. She didn't even ask questions, but her eyes held Nell's and her gaze never wavered. In the silence, Bunty waited for the question she knew would come.

It came.

"Why? Why is he doing this, Bunty? Why the lies? The false image? God knows, he has a lot going for him. Good looks, good background, wealth. It's true that he didn't always make the best choices, but, I don't know—could it be possible that he actually thinks this stuff is true?"

Bunty considered.

"It could be, but that would indicate a real pathology, so I'd say probably not," she said. "He knows it's not true—at least at some level he knows it. But he's probably been living like this for most of his life. When things got too painful, he figured out how they should have been and then lived those scripts in his mind. He probably figured he deserved better than he got. How could a great kid like he was have such a cold bastard for a father? How could one so intrinsically good deserve to see his mother die? Yes, he had a handsome trust fund from his grandmother, but that wasn't enough. Why did his father cut him off? Ergo, why didn't his father love him? It's complicated."

But Nell still wasn't satisfied.

"But Bunty, he opened himself to discovery. By calling me in and hiring me to write this book, he's exposing himself. He's inviting me in. Did he think I wouldn't uncover this?"

Bunty's smile was enigmatic.

"Perhaps he knew you would."

∾

Chapter 35

"Nell!" Deke's voice on the phone was ebullient. "Kid, it's great! I love it! I can't believe how you've gotten right down into the—well, the guts of the thing and brought it all out. I tell ya, I was right back there on 9/11, reliving the whole drama."

"I am gratified," Nell told him. "It is always very warming when a client likes the work.

"Oh, it's not perfect yet," Deke hurried to say. "We've got some work to do on changes. Tweaks. Those sorts of things, but for a first go this is pretty damn close. So let's set a time to get together and go over the revisions and edits I'd like to see."

"Fine. Let me grab my calendar and..."

But Deke interrupted himself. "Oh, gosh, wait! There's something I want to ask you first. Invite you to, rather. And I want you there! I want you to be in the audience for this!"

There was to be an awards banquet, Nell was told. Some variety of civic organization on the North Shore was presenting Deke with a Humanitarian of the Year Award—a black tie affair at a hotel in Salem, apparently—and Deke wanted a claque of admirers in attendance.

"So you can all applaud loudly," he joked. "Say you'll come. I

148

want you to see me in all my glory."

"Modest individual," Nell thought as she hung up the phone. But she had said yes.

≈

Chapter 36

PJ Morrissey was the name that flashed up on the Caller I.D. Surprised and curious, Nell picked up on the second ring.

"Ms. Bane? It's Patty Morrissey. I probably shouldn't be calling you, you know, at home and all. But I've thought about calling for a long time and have been sort of afraid to. Call, I mean."

"Patty, I don't know what it is you have to say, but I think I'd be very interested to hear it. And please—call me Nell."

"Oh. Alright. Nell, then. You sure this is a good enough time to talk? I mean, I can call back later if you..."

"Please—it's a perfect time. Patty, you sound as if you have something difficult you want to discuss."

"Oh, yes, I do!" Relief fled into the younger woman's voice. "Ms. Bane—Nell—I saw your name on the guest list for the banquet—the one honoring Mr. Kernow—and I knew I couldn't put this call off any longer."

Nell waited.

"Well, the thing is, I don't think the people who give out these awards to Mr. Kernow really have any idea who they're giving awards to."

"Go on," said Nell guardedly.

"Well, I'm not saying that The Children of Woe Fund doesn't do good works. It helps some people and all, but the one the Fund helps most is Mr. Kerow. Oh, and Mr. Zayder—he gets a lot of what you'd call 'help' too."

Nell was silent. Then she spoke very gently.

"Patty, I think it took a lot of courage to make this call—to share what you know with someone else. I think you might be describing some sort of embezzlement. Skimming, perhaps. But in any case, it's illegal and it is very serious, especially when the victim is a charity. You've had this knowledge for some time haven't you?"

"Well...I guess so."

"And what's prompting you to speak up now?"

"I don't know, I guess I've just had enough."

"Enough. Enough of?"

"Sitting here day after day," Patty spat out. "Sitting here and watching the money people give in good faith to a cause that is completely legitimate and worthwhile and they don't know—these people—that their money isn't going where they think it's going. That it isn't doing what it should. It's going, well, its going right into Mr. Kernow's back pocket. Into his house and his fancy car and meals in fancy restaurants for all his friends. And all the while, people are saying to him, 'oh, Mr. Kernow, you are so wonderful to be helping these poor, innocent children who have lost a parent.'"

Patty Morrissey's tirade finally ran out of steam. Nell heard a sort of gasp that could have been a sob.

"Patty. Listen to me. This is serious stuff to say. How do you know it? What have you seen?"

Patty Morrissey seemed to have regained her self-control. She spoke now with the chill sparseness that Nell knew from her first encounters with Miss Dry Ice.

"I know what goes on in the office even if they think I don't.

They think they're hiding stuff, but I know. I see. I know the money that comes in. Not all of it, of course, but enough. And I see the bills too—the bills Mr. Zayder handles—and I know things are not right!"

"And why did you decide to say something to me? There are authorities you could go to, you know. The FBI, for example.The attorney general, most certainly. Maybe the IRS if you suspect tax fraud. Why me?"

"Someone should know," Patty repeated miserably. "The people who give out awards don't seem to pay any attention. But you're writing this book about how great Mr. Kernow is. And you're going to that banquet and you're going to sit there applauding when Mr. Kernow gets his award and makes his speech. *Some*one should know. *You* should know!"

"Patty," Nell said, "I think you are very brave. This was a hard thing to say. And now I *do* know. I don't know just yet what I'll do about it—I can't even imagine what I *can* do about it—but I promise you I'll go to that banquet and while I sit there in that room, one person will know that Deke Kernow isn't who he says he is."

Chapter 37

"Nell," Robert shifted uncomfortably, "I may hate myself for what I'm about to say—because I despise rumors and the people who spread them—but I've heard a rumor. I heard it a while ago and didn't mention it, but now I feel I have to. It may be a matter of safety."

Nell stared at him. It was out of character for the urbane and polished Robert Hutchins to look so discomfited.

"Robert, you're positively squirming," she told him.

Robert continued as if he hadn't heard her.

"As I say, this is a crumb of G2 that I picked up at a charity event a few weeks ago. It wasn't a Children of Woe fund-raiser, by the way, but a lot of the same people show up at all these things. A small group was talking about Deke—and not in the most flattering terms, may I say—and one of them mentioned that his second wife had put a restraining order on him. Apparently our boy has a terrible temper, enough to provoke physical violence."

Nell stared.

Robert hastily raised his hands as if backing away from his story.

"Now I'm not saying this is true, mind you. It's just what I heard. Gossip, is all. Probably just the buzzing from a jealous..."

"No, Robert," Nell whispered. "I don't think so. I think that rumor may just be true."

And she told him about seeing the Third Mrs. Kernow's bruised jaw and swollen eye.

~

Chapter 38

When she had received Deke's invitation to attend the award banquet, she'd taken the little black dress out of the closet and regarded it without enthusiasm. Since meeting Deke Kernow, the LBD had seen more service than it had in the three years she'd owned it. Then, staring at it dangling from its padded hanger, she'd made a sudden decision. She would have a new dress! Something that didn't blend into the background for a change. Something smart. Snappy. She regretted that impulse now, but when the inspiration was fresh, Nell had realized she didn't know where to start acquiring such a dress. She thought of asking Bunty to join her on a shopping excursion and quickly dismissed the idea. Bunty's idea of a snappy outfit was a caftan from 1977. Instead, she called Ann Fitzmaurice and threw herself upon Ann's considerable sense of style.

Ann took her firmly in hand, and after a full afternoon of sorting industriously through shops and racks (Ann) and executing twists and tuggings in small fitting rooms (Nell), the two women emerged triumphant with a three-piece outfit that featured a long, flowing skirt, a sparkly top and a sort of jacket that dipped to the knee. Even Bunty, summoned to the impromptu fashion show, was impressed.

Ann, as a finishing touch—and in Nell's opinion, a very grand gesture—insisted on lending her jet and diamond earrings.

Nell protested.

"They're too precious, and besides, I never wear drops. They catch on things like my coat collar."

But Ann stood her ground.

"You need some bling," she told Nell, "besides, the jet will look terrific with your feathery, silver hair."

And so Nell—wearing bling, of all things—made her way to the distinguished old hotel on Salem's Common for the North Shore group's fete honoring one of its philanthropic businessmen. Nell had always felt comfortable in this hotel. From time to time, its face got treated to a lift but a patina of timelessness still showed through.

Nell was escorted to the VIP table and introduced to several tablemates. She was surprised, and a little unsettled, to see the Third Mrs. Kernow seated directly opposite her. Nell offered a tentative smile, which the 3MK appeared to look straight through.

"Nell Bane." Nell persevered. "We met briefly at your home."

When there was still no light of recognition, Nell blundered on.

"I'm working with your husband. On a book."

"Darling!" interrupted a woman who materialized suddenly at the 3MK's shoulder. "We missed you at the Snodgrass affair!"

As Deke's wife turned to speak to this stranger, Nell took the opportunity to examine her jaw for bruises. Was that just a trace of fading yellow beneath the skillfully applied make-up?

But here came the guest of honor himself, all jolly and back-slapping and hail-fellowing.

"Nell!" he cried, spotting her. "Marvelous. Everyone, I want you to meet the woman behind my success. This is the lady who's going to take me all the way to Hollywood, by God!"

Nell was embarrassed. Surely the woman behind any man's success should be his wife. Had she been the 3MK, she'd be crushed. And probably furious.

Nell reached for her water goblet and took a sip, quietly studying Deke's wife over the rim of the glass. All this time, and Nell still hadn't been properly introduced by name.

As hotel banquet fare went, this meal was better than most. Nell sportingly made her way through most of the fruit cup, the Caesar salad, the prime rib and baked potato and was regarding a slice of baked Alaska and wishing for strong, black coffee, when the master of ceremonies finally stood and tapped his knife on his water glass.

"Attention! Attention everybody. Come to attention now!"

He seemed very pleased with himself, and Nell knew they were about to experience an over-long introduction larded with homegrown humor.

"Coffee, ma'am?" a waitress asked in her ear.

Nell could have kissed her.

The M.C.'s wasn't the only speech. Several other members had quite a lot to say. Everyone spoke glowingly of Deke Kernow and his generosity, his tender-heartedness, his selfless humanitarianism.

Nell's foot went to sleep. The 3MK, she noticed, looked bored.

Then the guest of honor stood to prolonged applause. He smiled. He ducked his head modestly. Finally, he made the sort of crowd-hushing motions that quarterbacks make just before a snap.

A woman next to Nell leaned across the table and addressed the 3MK confidingly in a stage whisper.

"You must be *very* proud!"

The 3MK looked at her for a long moment.

"*Very*," she said.

To Nell's ears, the answer ponged of sarcasm, but the woman who'd spoken settled back in her chair looking satisfied.

A plaque was presented to Deke. Hands were shaken. Photographs were posed for. Smiles were ordered frozen in place with cries of "Cheese!"

"No, no!" someone coached from the audience, "say 'Money'!"

Much laughter. Nell's mouth felt stretched. She thought of the long, dark drive home to Newburyport that waited her at the end of this night.

Now Deke was speaking. Nell, who hadn't been listening closely, tuned in. He was talking about Rose Soon. Her jaw dropped slightly. His voice caught with emotion. He actually had to stop speaking, so overcome was he by the memory of carrying this woman through the streets of New York. He dropped his head and swallowed hard, trying to regain his composure.

The audience stirred a little in sympathy, then one helpful soul began to applaud and others quickly took it up. Someone noisily pushed back a chair and stood. A few others, eager to be part of this, jumped to their feet as well, and then, one by one, others slowly rose and stood applauding.

But Nell couldn't make herself rise. It felt like she was enchanted into the frozen pose of a seated statue. It seemed to her that she was the only person who hadn't joined the standing ovation. Well, she and the woman across the table—the Third Mrs. Kernow. If Patty Morrissey had been there, she would have made three.

～

Chapter 39

Nell drove toward Newburyport in a state of high disgust that mounted with each mile the odometer registered. The whole thing—the entire evening—had left a bad taste. A bad smell. All of it! The fawning, obsequious guests, the self-congratulatory demeanor of the hosts and speakers, the woman next to her at the table who was so eager to place herself forward by currying favor with the Third Mrs. Kernow, Deke's acceptance speech—a marvel of phoniness—and even herself. She was especially disgusted with herself. There she had sat, wearing a silly, expensive gown purchased just so she would blend with the donors and acolytes of a man who wasn't who he ought to be. And she must have *wanted* to blend. How had she wanted to be part of something she so despised?

"There now!" exclaimed Nell. "I'm judging! It's come to that!"

And her self-disgust deepened.

Whether it was the disgust or the rich beef, Nell felt quite ill by the time she returned home, and the feeling of dyspepsia continued into the next day. Lethargic and depressed, she wore her bathrobe late into the morning. She brewed a pot of tea, her mother's remedy for any ailment, and tried to warm her fingers by clutching the mug.

"You're not up yet? My God!" Bunty, banging through the back door, was shocked.

Nell turned her wan face in Bunty's direction.

"I wanted to find out how the dinner went," Bunty explained. "I was going to ask if you were the belle of the ball, but from your face—which looks like milk gone sour, by the way—I guess it didn't go all that well."

"I suppose it depends on who you are," Nell sighed. "The guest of honor had a whale of a time. So did all the shirts who got to stand up and gush about him. In fact, the only outliers were the Third Mrs. Kernow and me. Bunty, David Kernow is a phony. It's one thing to live a lie but it's another thing to promote it—to allow others to buy into it."

"Is there any more tea in that pot?"

Bunty peered into the big ceramic teapot, then helped herself to a mug from the cupboard, slopped out a mug-full and thumped down across from Nell.

"What're you going to do now?" she asked.

Nell sighed again.

"I have no idea."

But Nell really didn't feel well. Whether it was depression or the flu, she couldn't tell, but for three days she wafted about the house and everything looked gray. She phoned Deke Kernow to beg off the appointment they had made to go over the revisions to the manuscript draft. Using the excuse of the flu, Nell pushed the meeting out until the following week, and when Deke discovered he would be away on a trip for much of that week, their meeting went out even farther. Nell was relieved. Hanging up the phone, she discovered she was feeling better.

"Well, that should tell me something," she murmured.

But she knew she had to get busy.

⁓

Chapter 40

"Robert, I need a sounding board," she had said. "Would you like to apply for the position?"

So now she was seated in one of the comfortable chairs that flanked Robert's Beacon Hill fireplace. She was holding a very civilized glass of sherry and was pouring out to Robert all her concerns and discoveries about Deke Kernow. How could a guy who claimed to be such a humanitarian—someone so touched and moved by the human suffering of the likes of Rose Soon— how could this man treat the people closest to him not like people but like objects? No names, just labels. He acted as if they were nothing more than chattel there to make his life comfortable.

And that wasn't all! His life was a lie! His MIT background, his technical accomplishments, the companies he'd supposedly started and made successful. And the whole 9/11 thing—staying with the Altmans, the phony appointment in the North Tower and Rose Soon—especially Rose Soon—all fiction. And there were other things too—the hints of abuse his wives had suffered and the references Patty Morrissey had made about misuse of the charity's funds.

"It's all too much, Robert," Nell declared in summary. "It's more than I can simply and quietly bear."

Now she leaned forward toward him with her elbows on her knees, turning the delicate sherry glass between her fingers.

"If I go forward with this book, that makes me an accomplice. Deke Kernow is a man with no ethics, and if I participate in this book, knowing what I know, then I have compromised my ethics also."

Robert was horrified.

"Nell. What are you thinking of doing? Abandoning the project? Quitting?"

Nell nodded grimly. "Exactly that."

"But—you have a contract. Do you proposed to break it? *That's* hardly ethical."

"Robert, I have thought about this and thought about it. For a week and a half it's all I've thought about. As I see it, I have three choices. One, I could go ahead and finish up the book; I could take the final one-third payment, shut-up, turn my back, and try to forget the whole thing. Two, I could quit—break the contract— and return the first two-thirds of the money that Deke has paid me. Three, I could blow the lid off his story. Let it be known that he is a phony, a fraud."

"Be a whistleblower, you mean," supplied Robert.

"Yes."

Robert shook his head.

"I don't like options two and three, Nell. You've spent time— hours and hours of time. And you've brought your considerable talent to the project. Why would you give back the money that you have legitimately earned?"

"Because I'm pretty sure those checks Deke wrote to me came almost directly out of The Children of Woe Fund. I have accepted ill-gotten gains."

Robert snorted derisively. Nell was surprised. She had never heard Robert snort.

"Nonsense!"

"Listen, Robert, people gave money thinking they were contributing to a very worthy cause. They wanted those children of the 9/11 victims to have help. If I keep the money, it's almost as bad as simply shutting up and writing the book."

Robert shook his head again, but he persevered.

"Okay, let me address the third option you mentioned. The whistleblower thing. I don't think you should do that. I don't *want* you to do it."

"And why is that?"

But Robert only pinched his mouth into a grim set.

"Because it might be dangerous," he admitted finally.

"Robert...? Is there something more I should know?"

"Deke Kernow can be a charming man," Robert said slowly. "But you have only seen the charming side. Oh, I know, I know, there've been glimpses. His treatment of Patty Morrissey, his attitude toward his wife—but I think our boy is quite capable of a rage that goes beyond anything you've ever witnessed, Nell. I don't think you can even imagine what he may be capable of doing. And if you threaten to blow his cover, you could be in considerable trouble for your pains."

Robert passed his hand over his eyes and sat still for a few moments.

"Now I want to know what you are going to do. Have you decided?"

Nell was silent.

"I'm going to think some more, I guess. I'll let you know what I decide, when I decide."

"I want you to do that," Robert said. "I'm very serious, Nell. I care about you a great deal—you know that—and I'm asking you not to do anything without running it by me. Deal?'

"Oh!," she exclaimed, annoyed. "Oh, okay. Deal."

Chapter 41

Nell retreated into her usual therapy. Perhaps Bunty would have diagnosed it as denial, but Nell preferred to think of soup making as a way to focus on something constructive while leaving her subconscious alone to wrestle with its demons. Or its angels. And so she flipped through the pages of her recipes to find one that demanded a lot of ingredients but would yield a big bowl of comfort food. Ah. Vegetable soup with pesto would do it.

GOOD OL' VEGETABLE SOUP UPDATED

1 cup navy beans, rinsed
1 bay leaf
1 teaspoon fresh thyme
2 medium leeks, washed and finely chopped
2 medium carrots, diced
1 large potato, peeled and diced
1 32-oz can of whole tomatoes
2 cups of chicken broth
4 oz. of green beans, cut in pieces
1 small zucchini cubed

1 cup of frozen peas
1 teaspoon coarse salt
8 cups of cold water
1 container of purchased pesto

With a satisfying rattle, Nell flung the navy beans into the stockpot and covered them with about 6 cups of cold water. Once the beans had reached a brisk boil, she slid the pot off the heat and allowed the beans to bask in their warm bath for an hour. Then she drained the beans, returned them to the pot and drenched them with 3 cups of cold water, tossed in the bay leaf and thyme and brought the beans up to a boil again. There they simmered them until they were barely tender.

After another hour or so, Nell added the leeks, carrots, potato, tomatoes and her homemade chicken stock along with 2 more cups of water. The soup simmered and murmured away for almost another hour before Nell added the green beans, peas, and zucchini. When this second round of vegetables was just tender, Nell judged the soup ready to serve, so she stirred in the salt and several grinds of pepper, and ladled up a handsome bowlful which she topped it with a generous dab of pesto.

As she dipped her spoon into the soup, she allowed her mind to wander back to the ethical problem she had landed on herself. She had three options—none of them attractive.

If she chose the first, she would essentially do nothing. Or looked at another way, she would put on blinders and plod forward to the end of the book project. She would take the rest of her money and scarper. Her bank balance would benefit but what payment would her conscience demand?

The second option—the choice to take the high moral road—

would buy off her conscience. She considered what Robert had said about the work she had done so far. She had worked in good faith. Had believed in her client and had found no reason to doubt his story—at least not at first. Didn't that justify pocketing the money? Well, maybe not the last third that was still due, but hadn't she earned the first two-thirds? But her conscience spoke to her critically: "You know the money you received was obtained fraudulently. It was money extorted by lies from people who wished to give to charity. Aren't you participating in the lie if you don't give it back?"

Or, as a third option, she could chose to be a whistleblower, wasn't that what Robert had called it? She could go public and expose The Children of Woe Fund as a fraud. Pull the plug on the foundation. What would that result bring? Well, it would mean that no future contributions would come to Children of Woe. "And remember" whispered the little voice of confusion, "not all the money in the fund was mishandled; some of it went where it was supposed to go!" But option three would also expose Deke Kernow and Ira Zayder. Open them up to public disgrace and probably prison time. They would certainly be charged with repaying the funds they'd misappropriated.

Three choices. Nell went over them, then over them again. She tried making a chart that listed the options and the pros and cons of each—a sort of ethical risk analysis exercise. But the ethical probabilities were too complex to be reduced to a simple chart, and in the end, Nell felt no closer to a decision than she had when she'd started pulling together the ingredients for the soup.

Her soup bowl was empty. Nell sighed as she looked at the spoon resting against the edge of the bowl. Maybe a long walk on the beach would help.

∽

Chapter 42

The skinny, eleven-mile barrier island known as Plum Island, stretches south from the Merrimack River with Plum Island Sound on the landward side and the Atlantic Ocean and Great Britain on the other. Ipswich's Crane's Beach, just opposite the island's tip is no more than a minute away as the seagull flies, but by car, it's a half-hour or more. Plum Island was an easy drive for Nell, just out Water Street.

She had the beach to herself. For one thing, it was a weekday morning, and for another, it was cold. Damn cold, and a capricious wind was gusting off the Atlantic side. The mean wind made her nose run and her eyes stream, but Nell didn't care. With her hands shoved deep in her pockets, she strode along, weighing her options and looking for some clear signal that would lead her to the right choice. A seagull mocked her. She looked up.

"I deserve that," she said.

But she had delayed her meeting with Deke for as long as possible, and the appointment they'd agreed upon for Thursday was coming up fast. Moreover, she owed Robert a phone call. She'd promised to call. But even now she wasn't sure what she'd do. So she strode on.

Chapter 43

"I know what I'm going to do, Robert."

Nell was calm and decisive. She tried to picture Robert on the other end of the phone line, sitting beside his fireplace on Beacon Hill.

"And that would be what?" he asked.

"I am going to see Deke," Nell said firmly. "I'm going to keep the appointment we set, but instead of working on the revisions to the manuscript, I am going to resign. I plan to tell him face to face what I've discovered—or most of it anyway—and I'm going to say that my own ethics would be seriously compromised if I continued to work on this project. Knowing the lies that he intends to publish, I can't allow my name to be connected with the book."

This declaration was met with silence.

"Your name won't really be on the book," Robert, ever practical, pointed out. "You're the ghostwriter and to all practical purposes for publication, invisible."

"It will be there in essence," Nell said in a high-minded tone.

Then in a more pragmatic voice, she continued, "And, I'm going to give him a check for all the money he has advanced."

Now Robert grew animated.

"Nell! No! I can't let you do that! You legitimately earned that money. You didn't know the true story when you accepted the checks, and it's—what?—five months worth of hard work. No, that's going entirely too far!"

Nell was struck.

"Robert. You're right. If I give that money back to Deke, it won't do any good at all. It would just recycle back into the column of ill-gotten gains and Deke would spend it on something else. I will give it to a legitimate charity instead—there are hundreds dedicated to helping families 9/11 victims. I've seen them on line. Plenty of them are legitimate."

"Nell," Robert sounded exasperated, "that isn't what I meant. Bear with me here. I'm going to explain what's wrong with your plan."

Nell waited.

"In the first place, if you give away the money, Deke still has the book. He has the draft of a manuscript that isn't yet perfect but it is close enough for him—or for someone else—to finish it. Walking out on the job isn't going to stop publication of the lies. All it will do is deprive you of what you rightfully earned."

"If Deke hires someone else to finish the book," Nell argued, "that's his business, but that's beyond my control. This is a matter of ethics—mine. I have to live with myself."

"Okay, okay, let's just let that argument stand for a minute," Robert said. "Now I want you to think—just try to imagine—what Deke is going to say or do when you stand there in his study and make your little speech."

Nell didn't say anything.

Robert prompted her. Goaded her.

"Go on, think! What's going to happen? Well, let's look at what *could* happen. Is Deke going to be pleased?"

"No," Nell said honestly.

"What do you think he'll say? Or do?"

"I've no idea." Nell was growing tired of this guessing game. "I'll just speak my mind and leave. I'm not paying a social call. I don't intend to hang around."

"Deke Kernow has always been very pleasant to you," Robert said, refusing to be put off, "but I have reason to believe he has a very dark side—an angry side, possibly a violent side—and I'm not sure he wouldn't use it on you."

"I'm not going to blow the whistle on him," Nell pointed out. "I'm just inviting myself out of the equation, and as far as I'm concerned, he can keep the manuscript and do what he likes with it."

"But he doesn't know you're *not* going to blow the whistle," Robert argued. "His word isn't his bond—why should he think yours would be? Actual truth here isn't going to matter, Nell. It certainly hasn't up to now."

"Robert, I hear what you're saying. I know you are concerned for me and about me. But this *is* about me and it *is* what I'm going to do."

"When?"

"Thursday. We're scheduled to meet at eleven on Thursday."

"Then if you are bound and determined to go through with this, Nell, let me go with you."

"What? To act as my second? To slap your gloves across his cheeks if he insults me and cry, 'Fie on you sir! We'll meet at dawn'? Thank you, Robert, but no. This is my decision and it's my job to do."

"I'm the one who introduced the pair of you, remember? I have some skin in this game too—some responsibility in this mess. I'm coming with you!"

Nell had never known Robert to be so adamant, so agitated.

"Alright. We'll compromise. You can go to Lexington on Thursday, but we'll go in separate cars. You take your own car and sit outside in it while I meet with Deke. And if you see smoke rise or hear screams, you can burst in like Galahad or Bruce Willis or whomever and throw me over your shoulder and carry me to safety."

"Nell, that isn't funny. And I still don't like this, but I do insist on going, and I will be in Lexington, parked near the house, around eleven in the morning on Thursday."

"Robert, did I ever tell you that you are very dear?"

∾

Chapter 44

"Robert put the whammy on me." Nell murmured as she steered down the highway.

And Robert's warning ratcheted up her annoyance with each mile the Saab ate up. But she took time to notice—curiously—that it was Robert, not Deke, who was the target of her anger.

"Well then," Nell said out loud, "that isn't sensible. What *is* going on here?"

Fear, she realized as she drew along-side one of the signs for Lexington, was the culprit working here. It was fear that had caused the misalignment of emotion and had turned her anger onto the innocent messenger. She hadn't wanted to hear Robert say that Deke could be dangerous. She didn't want to think that he might do her physical harm, even with the 3MK's bruised jaw and blackened eye as possible evidence.

Once she'd admitted to herself that she was afraid—afraid that Deke might react violently when she delivered her news—her emotion shifted. She felt a flash of love for Robert, but the flames of nervousness were already licking up and the closer she got to Lexington, the higher they leaped.

Nell saw no sign of Robert's car when she turned onto Deke's street, but as she rolled around the curve of the road, she was brought up short. Blue lights and red ones flared and swirled, broadcasting emergency. The street in front of the house, as well as the driveway, was parked out with vehicles from the Lexington police and fire departments. Nell gasped. Her heart pounded. She pulled close to the curb and shaking, pushed her way out of the car.

A uniformed cop, standing in the street at the mouth of the driveway, held up a forbidding hand.

"Sorry, ma'am. I can't let you go any farther."

"But..." Nell started to argue, "but I have an appointment with..."

She realized how inane that sounded, and the cop just shook his head.

"Sorry. No farther."

"But what has happened?"

Her question earned another shake of the head.

"Not at liberty to say. There's been some trouble is all."

Nell looked past his shoulder. The front door was propped wide open and now she could see several EMTs maneuvering a stretcher in the front hall.

"Shooting," she heard someone announce.

A man whom Nell took to be a neighbor appeared beside her. Things were happening as if in a dream. His wife was suddenly there too.

"Yes! We heard shots!" she said excitedly.

"Not *shots*," her husband corrected her sharply. "We heard one shot."

The wife was not to be put off.

"Well, I heard several," she insisted.

One of the EMTs, backing through the door, was heard to say: "Steady there, Mike!"

And as one, Nell, the cop, and the neighbor couple turned to look.

A gurney with a great bundle strapped to it was being guided down the steps and then to the front walk. Suddenly Nell felt an arm around her. She turned quickly. Robert was beside her and just behind his shoulder she saw Jerry Gasso.

"Who is it?" inquired the neighbor wife excitedly.

"I think it's the wife," her husband told her.

"Oh God, Robert," Nell turned her face into Robert's shoulder. "He's shot her."

Robert patted her absently, his eyes still on the scene before them.

The spectators were silent as the bundle was loaded almost tenderly into the back of the ambulance. It took several minutes before the EMTs slammed themselves in. The vehicle backed slowly out of the driveway. Its red lights began to swirl but it made no sound. No siren mourned as the ambulance slowly—and rather majestically, Nell thought—traveled down the street toward whatever was its destination.

Another cop, shorter and fatter than Nell's guard—began stringing yellow crime tape around the property.

Nell's eyebrows went up. "Robert, what does that mean?"

But Robert had no answer. He stepped up to the guardian cop now and addressed him in a low, respectful tone.

"Do we know the victim's identity? The lady," he indicated Nell with a nod, "is quite alarmed. She had a meeting scheduled with Mr. Kernow this morning, and any information you can share would be appreciated."

"There are still a lot of unknowns," the cop told him. "The force will be here for quite a while working to sort matters out."

"But the victim..." Robert pursued the issue and received a firm shake of the head for an answer.

With a small shrug, Robert returned to Jerry and Nell, and the three continued to stand in the road watching, although there was little to see. The police action, whatever it involved, was now being conducted inside the house. Nell pictured the cops moving around the prized mid-century furniture with measuring tapes. She thought of the Fiestaware-colored lamps and the Poul Kjaerkholm bench of which Deke was so proud.

A car approached—a white Cadillac Escalade—and brakes screeched. A car door banged. And the Third Mrs. Kernow bounced out and strode toward to the driveway cop.

Nell put her hand over her mouth.

"Robert," she breathed, "it wasn't her!"

They watched the cop and the 3MK speaking for a few moments, and as they watched, they saw the cop put his arm around her and guide her slowly into the house.

"That was her!" the neighbor wife told her husband accusingly. "You said it was the wife, but it's not!"

The man did not reply.

"It must have been him, then!" the wife continued.

"Joan, your powers of deduction amaze me," said the sarcastic husband.

But Joan seemed immune to sarcasm, and she continued to peer toward the house with an avidity that Nell resented. Then she had to retrench.

"We're no better," she thought humbly. "Jerry and Robert and I standing here staring like voyeurs at a drama we don't even understand."

"It'll be alright, Nellybean," Jerry touched her arm consolingly.

Nell managed a wan smile in his direction.

"I appreciate that, Jerry. I just want to know what happened."

A police lieutenant, a man in middle age wearing a white hat and an obvious air of authority, stepped out on the porch and spoke with the driveway guardian who nodded and went inside. Robert approached this man, and Nell watched them speak for a few minutes. They were having, she noted, an actual conversation;

Robert wasn't simply being told to keep his distance. The pair was nodding now and by inches, drawing a distance between them, and Nell knew they were concluding the conversation. Robert raised his hand in a small salute of thanks and walked back down the driveway toward Nell and Jerry.

"It was Deke," Robert told them. "And it appears to be a suicide. I am so sorry, Nell."

And he folded her in his arms. But if he expected Nell to collapse or burst into tears, his expectation was not met. She allowed Robert to hold her but her eyes were dry. She was accepting.

"Thank you, Robert. I needed to know. And I'm sorry too— sorry for his wife and sorry for him."

She turned toward their cars, but Robert removed the keys from her hand and tossed them to Jerry.

"I'm driving you home, Nell, and Jerry can follow in your car. This isn't a good time for you to be alone and you aren't in the emotional shape to drive on the highway."

Nell started to protest that she could very well do it, then thought better of it. She would be grateful for the company— grateful to lean back, for once, and let others help her.

"Thank you," she said.

~

Chapter 45

The next days reminded Nell of running a low-grade fever. You try to go about the routine of your days, but something—something just below the surface—isn't quite right. Nell began to think she was obsessed. Variations on the scene at Deke's swam through her dreams, usually resembling nothing at all like the Lexington house, but Nell knew, no matter what the incarnation, that the house was Deke's, that the scene was Deke's and that the body on the gurney was her late client Deke Kernow. At Fowle's Market every morning, Nell was the first customer to grab *The Boston Globe,* but aside from a small article on page 2 the day after the event, there was no mention that a prominent philanthropist had been found dead in his Lexington home. And several times a day, Nell searched online, even checking the Lexington *Patch.*

Nothing. Mad for answers, Nell couldn't figure out why every door was closed. She called Robert daily. He and Jerry had stood with her as witnesses and now the three were bound psychologically in the way of people who have witnessed a horrific event—a battle in a war or the shared experience of a concentration camp. But Robert didn't have the answers she wanted either.

"When there's a suicide," he offered, "the police and press

are very reluctant to share details. Perhaps there's a pall of shame that hangs over a suicide, but that won't last forever. One of these days things will open up and we'll be able to get the answers."

Nell had a telephone call from an unexpected source. John Altman in New York had somehow heard the news and hoped Nell could enlighten him.

"I wish I could, John," she told him, "but I'm in the dark as much as you. I will call you though, when I know something."

Altman pursued the matter.

"Aren't there any funeral plans? There must be something."

"None that I know," Nell said sadly. "One of the hard things about a suicide is that the survivors have to try to make sense of it—understand it. That's what I've always heard anyway, and now I understand how frustrating it is. And how easy it is to blame oneself."

And truth be known, Nell felt a little ashamed of her mission to Lexington that morning. She'd been prepared to tell Deke she was backing away from the book, that she was breaking their contract. What if, she thought, what if she'd found him and told him that, then the next day he'd committed his act of self-terrorism? The very idea made her knees weak.

Finally, unable to stand the suspense, Nell drove to the Lexington police station and asked to see the lieutenant. After enduring some suspicious questions, she was finally granted an audience with the man she recognized from the driveway. She explained slowly and carefully, who she was and pleaded respectfully for more details.

"I understand it was a suicide," she said, "but I wondered if Mr. Kernow left a note."

He had.

Nell was dumbstruck.

"Might I...might I be allowed to see it? To know what it said?"

Well, no, the lieutenant was sorry but he couldn't allow her to see the note.

"Could you tell me to whom it was addressed?"

The lieutenant considered. "Perhaps at some point," he acquiesced, "but not right now. I'm sorry."

So was Nell. But knowing there was a note—that Deke had considered his action and wished to explain it, whetted Nell's curiosity. She knew, Pandora-like, that she couldn't leave this alone.

"If only I'd been there a day earlier," she mourned to Bunty, "perhaps I could have done something. Said something. Maybe picked up on a reference or a mood of depression and I could have..."

"Stop!" Bunty commanded. "Stop right there. That's exactly what everyone says when there's been a suicide. 'If only I could have been there, I could have stopped it.' Listen to yourself! I! I! This isn't about you—or about anyone else for that matter. Whatever motivated Deke to take his own life, it was his decision to do it and his alone. He picked the time and place, Nell. He chose the privacy of his own home and he did it when he was alone—when his wife was away."

Nell was slightly awed by Bunty's scolding logic.

"You complained that Deke Kernow was self-centered," Bunty told her. "That it was all about Deke. Well, isn't that what you're doing? You're placing yourself right on center stage. Nell—darling—you were only a bit player in Deke Kernow's movie. Or in anyone's movie, for that matter."

"Point taken," Nell said grudgingly. "Thanks for sobering me up, Bunty. But," she continued grimly, "I still intend to find out what happened, and I won't quit looking and asking until I do."

"Well, you just go ahead and do that, Pandora," was Bunty's parting remark.

∼

Chapter 46

Nell felt sad. And she felt the need to nourish herself. Nothing rich, nothing complicated, just something simple, ascetic and warm. Carrot Ginger Soup would suffice.

CARROT GINGER SOUP

2 T unsalted butter
1 large onion, diced
10-12 carrots, peeled and sliced
1-1/2 fresh chopped or grated ginger
4 cups of chicken broth

Nell sauted the onion in butter, stirring in the carrots, ginger and the broth, and then simmering the carrots to tenderness. She plunged the immersion blender into the pot to puree the soup and she tasted it for seasonings. No need for cream or orange juice. Feeding soul and body, Nell slowly consumed the carrot ginger soup and thought about everything. And tried to think about nothing at all.

Chapter 47

It was on the television news where the mystery began to crack. Nell could hardly believe it. She was half-dozing in front of the TV, waiting to hear the weather report at eleven o'clock, when the anchor read:

> *Ira Zayder of Watertown was arrested today, along with his nephew Richard Zayder, in connection with an extortion scheme designed to misappropriate funds from The Children of Woe Fund, a charity that helps the children of the victims of international terror. The fund was organized after 9/11 and in the last years its charitable contributions have taken on international scope.*

Nell had been curled on the sofa, sitting on her feet, but now her feet hit the floor with a thump, and she leaned toward the television, as though proximity would make the news more clear. The screen showed two men with their coat collars pulled high, being led out a door. Yes, Nell was pretty sure she recognized the ferrety little Ira Zayder. His companion, she supposed, was his nephew Richard. And was that the door of the office in Gloucester? Nell didn't think so. Watertown, apparently.

Rats! Was that going to be all? That's the trouble with the news, Nell fumed. They dangle a story in front of you, get you all hot and interested, then they go on to something else and leave you hanging. If Nell ever got the opportunity to produce a news show, she'd call it "Whatever Happened To..." And the whole point of her program would be to bring you follow-up to the stories you'd wondered about and invested time in following—stories that you really wanted to hear more about but never discovered how they turned out. It was so frustrating.

She grabbed the remote and clicked around the channels, trying to see if any other stations had picked up the story. She found nothing though. And in all the excitement of clicking and searching, never did get to hear the weather.

But the newspaper the next morning supplied more detail.

The F.B.I. yesterday seized the financial records of the charitable foundation called The Children of Woe Fund, an organization chartered to provide aid to the children of victims of international terrorism, specifically to the children of the victims of 9/11. These records, in conjunction with the charity's internal correspondence and employee interviews, indicated that the fund's founder, David Kernow, and its legal counselor/ business manager, Ira Zayder, colluded to divert monies from the funds into their private accounts. On Monday, Attorney Ira Zayder was arrested at his home in Watertown along with his nephew Richard Zayder, who managed the fund's website and telephone solicitation operations. David Kernow, the fund's founder, was discovered dead in his Lexington home last week. Suicide was the apparent cause of his death.

Following a tip regarding the misappropriation of charitable monies, the Channel 3 investigative news team was preparing to break the story. As well, the attorney general, the F.B.I. and the IRS had all stepped in to examine the books and practices of the organization.

It was noted that for four years, the charity had failed to file required federal and state reports showing the amounts of money the organization had received and how the funds were spent. This oversight put the charity's tax exempt status in jeopardy, and it is clear that donations intended to aid the children of 9/11 victims, as well as the offspring of other sorts of terrorism, were used to pay the credit card debts of Kernow and Zayder as well as a mortgage on Kernow's 6,200-square foot home in Lexington. Kernow was known for his lavish fund-raising parties to which wealthy donors vied for invitations, and he was regarded as a well-liked philanthropist who used his own funds, as well as his foundation's, to help in a popular cause.

Around the time The Children of Woe Fund was established, a number of similar nonprofits were set up—most legitimate—but some, especially those with online operations, were fraudulent. The misappropriation of charitable funds in this case, is one more example of the lax scrutiny on nonprofits, allowing the unscrupulous few to prey upon well-intentioned donors. One of the sad results, when news of this nature goes public, is that fewer dollars are released to charities because a jaded public can no longer trust donations to do the work they are meant to do.

Ira Zayder and Richard Zayder are due to appear in superior court next week for arraignment.

Nell read the article twice. She wondered if Deke had known that the F.B.I., the IRS and the Channel 3 investigative team were about to swoop down upon the headquarters of The Children of Woe Fund. Zayder, she noted, was picked up in Watertown, not in

Gloucester. But that didn't mean much—he wasn't in the office all that much at any time.

With time on her hands now and nothing to write, Nell decided to take a drive to Gloucester.

∾

Chapter 48

She wasn't sure what she expected to find. It's just that something was calling her to the charity's offices—maybe to have a word with Patty Morrissey or maybe just to see if the premises was draped with a padlock and chain, hung there by the F.B.I.

As she drove along Route 128, she replayed a conversation she'd had with Robert the day before.

"It is fortunate," Robert had remarked, "that you hadn't gotten to Deke in time to give back the money he paid you. What if you'd met with him, handed over your check and the next day he bumped himself off?"

"Robert!" Nell was scandalized, "I've never heard you talk like that."

Robert had chuckled.

"The criminal aspect of this event has brought it out, I expect. But I'm serious about the timing though. Now you don't need to worry about giving it back."

"It is still ill-gotten gains," Nell pointed out. "Anyway, I wasn't going to give it to Deke. I was going to find a deserving charity to give it to."

"You do realize," Robert said, "that restitution will be made for the funds that were misappropriated. Part of Zayder's sentencing—when it eventually comes along—will require him to pay back what he took, with interest and penalties. Whether he can do that or not is anybody's guess. But Deke's estate will probably be held liable as well. I expect to see that house in Lexington go on the market so the IRS can exact its pound of flesh."

"Robert! I just thought! What will happen to The Children of Woe Fund now?"

"Haven't a clue, Nell. It might be dissolved and any residual monies distributed, but it's useless to speculate. I really don't know."

Suddenly Nell thought about Patty Morrissey. Jobless again, poor kid. Patty was one of the reasons Nell was heading for Rocky Neck.

But hers was a fool's errand in the end. She parked her car once again in the lot and headed for the charity's offices on shank's mare. But the door to the staircase was locked. Nell tried to get around the building and see the office windows from the water side, but in that attempt, she was thwarted as well.

In the end, she reclaimed her car and bumped it down Pirate's Lane, parked in front of the North Shore Arts building, and stood looking across the harbor until she could pick out the windows of The Children of Woe Fund. The windows, she thought, looked blank like a sick individual with an empty, vacant stare.

≈

Chapter 49

"Like a moth to a flame," Nell murmured. "Like a dog returning to its vomit. Like a swallow flying toward Capistrano."

Could any of these clichés explain why she was drawn to Lexington and to the affairs of the late Deke Kernow? Continuing her internal conversation, she admonished, "This could be very awkward, Eleanor. Why can't you leave this alone?"

But she couldn't leave it. And when she learned that there was to be an interment of Deke Kernow's ashes, Nell felt she had to be there to stand as witness. No calling hours had been arranged at a funeral home or at the house. No memorial service either. Just this interment with whatever words would be read over the grave—or perhaps no words.

Nell found the cemetery and parked her car on the verge of one of the winding roads. Then she picked her way across the grass toward a knot of people she had spotted—stepping on tiptoe among the headstones, taking care not to make a disrespectful step nor let her heels sink in the soggy earth. Coming closer, she recognized the Third Mrs. Kernow in a long, black coat. Several people stood around her in attitudes of support. Her pit crew, thought Nell, then scolded herself for the rude thought. Relatives of the 3MK, Nell took them to be, and probably funeral personnel as well, and hopefully someone who would officiate at whatever ceremony the survivors had managed. It was, really, a pitifully small turnout. All the people who had hung on Deke at his parties, all the business associates he had worked with (and from whom he had cadged venture capital and charitable donations)—where were they? One man, however, was standing alone off to the side, clearly not a member of the 3MK's support group. Nell surmised he had some connection of friendship with Deke. She stepped next to him, and he glanced at her.

"Sad day," he remarked.

"It is."

They both faced front—or more accurately, faced the spot of anticipated action near the dug grave—and gazed self-consciously above it toward the line of trees beyond.

The man spoke again.

"Are you a friend of the family?"

"No," Nell said slowly, "I knew Deke actually. I was working on a project with him—a book project."

The man was surprised.

"You're Nell!" he told her. "Nell Bane, the writer."

He thrust out his hand.

"I'm John Altman."

It was Nell's turn for surprise.

"I didn't expect to see you here," she said shaking his hand. "You, of all people, have reason to feel very much fouled by Deke Kernow."

Altman shrugged. "I'm willing to let bygones be bygones. I prefer to remember the good times we did have, and I believe endings are important. I believe in saying proper good-byes."

But now a man disengaged himself from the black-clad knot and stepped nearer to the grave. Whether or not he was a cleric, Nell couldn't tell, but apparently he was going to do some sort of officiating. He cleared his throat.

"Ladies and gentlemen—friends, family—thank you for coming here today as we lay to rest our...our friend and husband, David Douglas Kernow."

A short man was making his hasty way toward them, swerving through the maze of headstones. Breathless, he caught up with the group and positioned himself on the other side of Nell.

"*Whew!*" he exclaimed softly, out of breath.

Nell glanced to her left. It was Gordon Porter.

She pondered the fact of his presence for several seconds, then focused again on the speaker who had quickened his pace and was finishing up his remarks in rather a rush. He nodded now to someone Nell couldn't see, and a cask was placed in his hands.

"Earth to earth" he intoned, "ashes to ashes, dust to dust."

The cask was gently set on the edge of the grave, and the mourners, as one, immediately turned away as if the vessel, the open grave, and the folds of green Astroturf were somehow indecent. Or maybe just embarrassing. A man had his arm around the 3MK now and on her other side, a woman walked, patting her hand. The widow didn't look grief-stricken, merely grim. She was borne away in the vanguard of the black-clad group toward the waiting cars. John Altman, Gordon Porter, and Nell remained respectfully in place, still facing front, until the little party had passed.

Gordon Porter was the first to speak.

"The poor son-of-a-bitch," he murmured.

Nell was struck. Suddenly she was in the barn again, sitting with Gordon under the haymow, watching Deke move through his party. It was Gordon who had first compared Kernow to Gatsby. And now, standing in this cemetery, Nell wondered if he had intentionally repeated the epitaph spoken by the Owl-eyed Man at Gatsby's grave.

She turned to Gordon.

"You're alone?"

"Yes, Helene wouldn't—*didn't*—want to come. She wasn't...well, she wasn't feeling well."

"You've read the papers," Nell said. "You surely know what happened—that The Children of Woe Fund was rancid with fraud?"

"Oh yes, I know. Maybe some of the money did some good though. Who knows? One hopes."

"Will you miss Deke's parties?" Nell smiled. "His fund-raisers?"

Gordon Porter grinned.

"What do you think? But there will be other parties. Helene will find other attractive hosts to fall in love with, other causes that need a Lady Bountiful. All is not lost—yet."

"Oh!" Nell said, "I'm sorry, please let me introduce you to an old friend of Deke's. John Altman, this is Gordon Porter, he donated handsomely to The Children of Woe Fund."

The men shook hands. Then the three of them stood awkwardly for a few seconds. Nell felt her high heels sinking slowly into the turf. What were they to do now?

But Altman decided for them. He sighed and looked at his watch.

"I've gotta get going. I'm catching the shuttle. Have to be in New York for a dinner thing."

He touched Nell's elbow.

"I want to read that book, though. You promised me a copy. First edition."

"There's not going to be 'that' book," Nell told him sadly.

"Sorry to hear it. What was it going to be called?"

"*Phoenix Ascending*," Nell told him. "It should have been called *Pack Of Lies*."

～

Chapter 50

Nell let her car roll slowly through the cemetery gates, but instead of turning onto Route 95, as she'd intended, she drove south on Bedford Street, aiming for the police station in the Center.

"You again," snorted the lieutenant, but he smiled when he said it.

"Yep," Nell agreed ruefully. "Me again."

The lieutenant stopped whatever he was working on, folded his hands on his desk and looked up at her.

"Have a seat," he said with exaggerated courtesy and he gestured grandly as if he were sweeping her toward the place of honor in an exclusive restaurant.

Nell sat.

"Well?" he prompted.

"I just wanted to see if I could talk you into releasing that note."

"You are going to haunt me until I show you, aren't you?"

"Yes."

The lieutenant snorted again but he opened his desk drawer and withdrew an envelope, which he passed across to her, saying, "Anything to get you out of my hair."

"May I have this?" she asked. "Or do I have to read it here?"

"Take it!" he gestured. "Be my guest. It's just a copy, and it isn't confidential any longer."

"Thank you."

Nell slipped the envelope into her bag and continued to sit. He had, after all, offered her the chair and she intended to make the most of it.

"Do you know what will happen to Mr. Kernow's wife?"

"I understand that she's leaving Lexington—has already left, in fact—perhaps to stay with friends or relatives. The force was asked to keep an eye on the property. I do have her address, but I doubt she'd want to be in touch with you or anyone."

Nell understood.

"Will the house go on the market?"

"Ultimately, it certainly will. But I would think it, along with other assets, will be entailed for some time to come."

Nell considered whether she had any more questions, and the lieutenant watched her carefully while she thought.

"Well, that about wraps it up, I guess," she said slowly.

He nodded. When he spoke again his voice was softer—the teasing crust of sarcasm was gone.

"Ms. Bane, I know Kernow was a friend of yours. I've observed that a lot of people who might have called him their friend were not around in the end. You are unique in your persistence—your damned persistence. I just want to say that I know you've had a loss too, and you have my sympathy."

"I just want to get at the truth."

"We have that in common," the lieutenant said.

"I really don't deserve any praise," she said honestly. "I was pretty disgusted when I found out about the fraud and embezzlement of his foundation."

The lieutenant nodded.

"Even so," he said.

~

Chapter 51

To Patricia Morrissey:

When you read this, I will no longer be living. My death will be—to a great extent—your fault. The Children of Woe Fund did much good in this sad world. One of the things it did was pay your salary, young lady, modest though it was. And how did you repay the hand that fed you? By going to the media, to that TV investigative guy, and blabbing about "practices" in the Fund which you didn't understand and which in your ignorance believed to be illegal. You and you alone, Patricia, set that pushy young, Channel 3 reporter on me. He hounded me like a dog after a rat. His car was parked outside my house at all hours. I couldn't go into a restaurant where I didn't see him. The pressure on me was terrible. The A.G. stuck her nose in, and now I've found out that the F.B.I. is in on this and so is the IRS. I will be ruined when this gets out! That's what you wanted, isn't it? To see me ruined! To see my reputation dragged through the mud! Well, The Children of Woe Fund will be bankrupt and it will be all over the papers and on the news and through the streets and this is your fault! The news is about to break...well, I won't be around to see it. You won't get your wish to humiliate me, but when you read this note and read the papers, I want you to realize what you have done. I want you to feel the shame of it!

Deke

~

Chapter 52

"I'm inviting you to a post-mortem, Bunty."

"What?' Bunty was considerably startled. "Whose?"

"Deke's. Robert and Jerry are coming up from Boston to talk things over and see if we can make any sense of it. You're invited to give expert testimony. There'll be lentil soup."

"Yum. I'll bring a bottle of Chateauneuf du Pape—Chateau Mont-Redon 2004, in fact."

"Bunty! That's awfully grand. It's just lentil soup."

"And good company. What time?"

The lentil soup was simmering on the Aga when Robert and Jerry, followed closely by Bunty, gathered in Nell's kitchen.

"Okay," Nell said, "the meeting will come to order. I guess the place to start is with The Note—Deke's final exit lines."

The others nodded and settled in, arranging themselves on the sofa and club chairs in the snug.

Nell gravely read the suicide note. Silence followed. She slowly turned to look at Bunty.

"Your comments, Dr. Whitney?"

"Please, I'm just a humble potter. But, okay, here are a few things I'm hearing. Deke was projecting when he wrote that note.

Projecting wildly. He couldn't bear to think of himself as less than the best little boy, so he tried pushing responsibility—or blame—outside himself and onto someone else. In that, his behavior was consistent. He couldn't accept being seen as less than perfect—even in his own eyes. He couldn't admit blame for any wrongdoing, so he projected it onto others—in this case, onto Patty. He addressed the suicide note to her. And I have to wonder if she had spoken to him about this or how he knew she was the whistleblower. But regardless of how he knew, it's clear that he saw the bomb rolling down the hill toward him. Hence, we can assume he was warned of the coming explosion, and he may have been warned by Patty herself. She may have told him that she was blowing the whistle. I'm not sure about that, though. If that were the case, he would have gotten furious at her and told her off face to face or even done her physical harm."

Bunty pondered this.

"Maybe she left a message in his voice mail," Jerry speculated helpfully.

"She could have," Bunty agreed. "We don't know. But we *do* know that Deke was tipped off in some way or by someone, that the investigative team, the attorney general, the F.B.I and the IRS were all about to descend."

"The trouble with this sort of thing," Nell complained, "is you unravel one thread and run right into a tighter knot."

"Well," Bunty continued, "it's helpful to understand why Deke felt driven to suicide when he understood that the bomb was about to detonate. Granted, no one is eager to face public humiliation and certain retribution, but few would be driven to such a dramatic and terrible extreme as suicide, correct? But Deke was different. And, again, he was consistent. He had to be the golden boy. The all-powerful one. Just as he couldn't face his own human-ness—and therefore had built a life on lies about who he was and what he'd accomplished—so was he unable to face the whole house of cards tumbling down. He couldn't face being exposed for the liar and fraud he was."

Nell was nodding.

"The shame," she said sadly. "The shame was too great for him to bear. But his suicide wasn't going to stop the scandal from breaking."

"No," Bunty agreed, "but it would stop him from having to see it. He wouldn't have bear witness."

Silence settled over the group again. Jerry stared into the fire. Nell stared at her lap. Robert studied the tips of his polished loafers. Bunty simply looked pensively into space.

Robert cleared his throat.

"Perhaps it will help if we leave this speculation for a while and see if another subject will ultimately shed light."

He pulled a couple of folded sheets of paper from his inside jacket pocket and frowned at them. The others waited.

"Nell, while you were trying to shake the suicide note lose from the Lexington police, I was trying to dig up more to the story about the fraud that was underway at The Children of Woe Fund."

He referred to his papers.

"There was fraud and misappropriation on several levels. As Patty Morrissey had observed, Ira Zayder was paying Deke's personal bills. Some reimbursement, of course, is completely legitimate. Travel expenses and that sort of thing. However, Deke was grossly exceeding the definition of legitimate, and it turns out Zayder was paying some of his own—Zayder's own—personal expenses as well. That's called misappropriation of assets. The Children of Woe Fund had the whole ball of wax—skimming, larceny, and cash misappropriation. Oh, and there were also incidences of fraudulent disbursements; that's when an organization pays expenses it actually doesn't owe."

Robert looked up over his glasses.

"There's more, unfortunately," he said. "As the papers stated,

197

the fund—administered by Ira Zayer, I assume—failed to file the reports required by the state and the federal government. Reports that show how much money the Fund received and how much it spent. This failure results in the loss of tax-exempt status, and that is very serious."

The others nodded. They'd understood that from the news reports.

"Zayder," continued Robert, "presumably with Kernow's knowledge, deliberately falsified the charity's financial statements. Financial statement fraud, I found out, is the most common type of fraud among nonprofits."

"Robert glanced down, prepared to read further.

"But wait!" murmured Jerry, "There's *more!*"

Robert looked at him.

"Sorry," Jerry mouthed.

"There's also a charge of internet fraud."

"*Internet* fraud?" echoed Nell. "How on earth does that come in?"

"Zayder reported that fees paid to telephone solicitors—this is one of the operations where young Richard Zayder was involved—were reported as program expenses."

"Is there anything more?" Nell asked weakly.

"Probably," Robert said drily. "I just got tired of sleuthing."

The four resumed their former occupations—Jerry gazing at the fire, Robert at his shoes, Nell at her lap and Bunty at some invisible plane of inner space.

But it was Bunty who finally spoke.

"I have a splendid bottle of wine," she said, "and I am prepared to uncork it and pass around the glasses. Enough speculation for now. There will be a lot more to come out later, I suspect."

"And I," announced Nell, "am going to give the lentil soup a turn with the spoon, and after we've had a glass of Bunty's splendid wine, we'll each have a bowlful."

HERE IS HOW NELL MADE THE LENTIL SOUP.

3 cloves of garlic, minced
1 teaspoon of olive oil
2 cups of Italian sausage, sliced into coins
8 whole cloves
1 medium onion
6 cups of chicken stock
2 cups of water
2 cups of lentils, rinsed and picked over
2 bay leaves
1/2 teaspoon of ground rosemary
Tabasco sauce to taste.

After Nell browned the sausages, she stirred the garlic
around in the pan for one minute. She added the stock
and water, then peeled the onion and studded it with
cloves. This she added to the sausage and stock, then she
spilled in the lentils, and added the bay leaves and the
rosemary. She watched while the stock grew to a boil,
then turned down the heat and allowed the pot to sit there,
simmering on the Aga until the lentils grew tender.

When Nell had ladled up the soup bowls, she passed around
the Tabasco and a basket of sourdough rolls.

∽

Chapter 53

On a quiet road off a side street west of Stoneham's Main Street, and situated amid a scumble of modest homes, Nell found Patty Morrissey's house. White vinyl siding, black plastic shutters and a child's faded plastic vehicle parked askew, or abandoned, beside the driveway. The young woman who opened the door looked different somehow from the person Nell knew from the Fund's office—the woman she'd privately named Miss Dry Ice.

"Hi," Patty pulled the door open wider in welcome. "There's still some morning coffee and I can nuke it for a second. Would you like some?"

Nell did not want a cup of coffee, not even freshly brewed coffee.

"I'd *love* some!" she declared and followed Patty down a narrow hall to the kitchen.

The kitchen, at the back of the house, was brighter than the hall—quite pleasant, really—and its window overlooked a backyard with a neatly edged garden and a high board fence.

"You want to stay in here?" Patty asked hesitantly, "or should we go into the living room?"

"This is perfect." Nell was emphatic. "I like kitchens, don't you? Much cozier."

As if to punctuate her conviction, she set her quilted bag down firmly on the floor beside one of the kitchen chairs and then placed her bottom on the chair's seat. She watched Patty collect mugs, milk and sugar, open a package of mini donuts and arrange these on a small plate. When all this clobber and the steaming mugs were on the table—Nell could smell the coffee's bitter strength—and when Patty had taken the chair opposite, Nell came to the point.

"I appreciate your willingness to see me," she said. "I'm sure all of these events—indeed the whole thing with The Children of Woe Fund—have been very difficult for you."

Patty nodded and looked down into the coffee's depths.

"You should know, I think," continued Nell, "that I was on my way to see Deke that morning he—the morning he died. I don't know, maybe if I gotten there an hour earlier, things might have been different. Probably not though. I don't mean to suggest that I could have prevented his suicide, and if things had been different for him, they might have been worse for me. And maybe for you. In any case, I want you to know that I think what you did was brave. Very courageous. You took some significant risks, and I am so glad you are safe."

Patty still didn't respond, but Nell had the impression she was listening intently.

"I wasn't going to blow the whistle on Deke outright," Nell continued, "but I was going to let him know that I knew him for what he was—a liar and a fraud. Furthermore, I was intending to resign from the writing job. I intended to give back the money he'd advanced. We were about two-thirds of the way through the ghostwriting project, you see, and he'd paid for two-thirds of the book."

Here Nell paused, waiting to see if Patty had anything to say, but the young woman held her silence. Nell gave it six beats, then plunged on.

"I am curious about a couple things though, and I wonder if you'd be willing to satisfy my curiosity?"

Patty looked up sharply. "Go on."

"Well, here's what I would like to know. When did you find out about the fraud within the foundation? Did you ever confront Deke with what you'd knew? And finally, but most importantly, why did you decide to blow the whistle and how did you know how to go about it?"

Patty Morrissey took a deep, slow breath.

"Wow," she whispered. Then slowly, "Well, okay, here's how I found out what was going on. I didn't like Mr. Zayder. He was mean and he was sneaky. He treated me like I was an air-headed twit, but I'm not stupid. I saw what envelopes came into the office and also saw the mail that was going out. I heard conversations that Mr. Zayder had with Mr. Kernow and I could hear what both said on the telephones. I was a human being with ears, not some cabinet or fax machine that was simply office equipment. I'm not blind, deaf nor stupid. I had suspicions at first, then I went looking for evidence. And I found it."

Patty looked thoughtful, then continued, addressing the next question.

"Did I go to Mr. Kernow and tell him what I knew? No. We didn't have that kind of relationship. It wasn't even a boss-employee relationship really—more like an overseer-slave relationship. He wasn't very nice to me, Mrs. Bane."

Patty looked Nell straight in the eye.

"He yelled at me, he belittled me, sometimes he was actually abusive."

Nell nodded.

"I know. I saw some of that. And it troubled me. It was one of the first signals to me that Deke Kernow was not the altruistic, caring individual he posed as. I thought that a man who could be reduced to tears by the plights of people he didn't even know would not be a man to treat those he *did* know so shabbily."

"There were times I almost hated him," Patty whispered. "By the time I decided to—as you put it "blow the whistle"—I believed he deserved everything he was going to get! If they gave him a jail sentence—fine. If they gave him a huge fine—a fine so big that it ruined him—even better. If they'd put him in the stocks or the pillory like they did in Old Salem, I'd have danced on the Common right in front of his face. He cared terribly what people thought about him, Mr. Kernow did. Public shame was what he deserved!"

Nell lifted her mug and attempted to sip the coffee. It was still scalding, and she set it down. She studied Patty's foreshortened face.

"Well, he's certainly not going to pay with jail time," she observed quietly, "and I can't comment on whether he's at peace now or not. I understand that his estate, or what's left of it, will go toward restitution. However, the IRS gets in line first for their pound of flesh, after that..."

Nell shrugged.

"Ira Zayder will certainly be cooling his heels in prison," she continued. "As well, he'll be held responsible for paybacks and fines. I doubt though that he will be able to fulfill that obligation. And the fate and future of The Children of Woe Fund is in limbo. I'm sure there will be audits and if there is anything left in the coffers, some judge will, in time, decide about them."

She stopped and looked at Patty

"I have one more question—this is the important one. I was worried about you, Patty, when I finally got to see Deke's suicide note. Did you know about that note?"

"Yeah. I read it. The police in Lexington—this nice lieutenant—he brought it over for me to read. Said he was real sorry to have to do it, but the note was addressed to me and all and so I had to see it."

She shook her head.

"I'm sorry you had to see it," Nell said softly. "When I finally got to see the note myself, and when I read it, I was very concerned about its effect on you. Did you feel in any way guilty?"

"Me? No! That's what he wanted me to feel, Mr. Kernow. He was treating me like crap all the way to the end. To *past* the end! He *wanted* to hurt me. But I'd made up my mind even before I called that reporter, that no more! I wasn't going to stand for any more from him, even if he was dead! So you know what I said, Mrs. Bane? Do you want to know?"

"Of course," Nell murmured.

"'You can't get me now, Mr. Kernow,' I said. 'You can threaten me, you can try to guilt trip me, but I don't have to accept any of it. And you didn't win. I win! I'm the last one standing.'"

Patty tossed her head triumphantly.

Nell smiled.

"And what about you now?" she asked softly. "What'll you do?"

Now Patty looked up and met Nell's eyes directly.

"Me? I go job hunting. It's okay, I've been meat on the market before. I'm good at what I do and I know it. And this time I'm not going to settle for the treatment I got in Gloucester. I'll demand respect, and I can do that because I've learned to respect myself. I learned that I can take a very risky step and act when action is called for. Going to the Channel 3 investigative team—that took guts. I was sick for weeks before I did it. Before I blew the whistle. But once I'd done it, I felt like a million bucks!"

Nell smiled at her and Patty returned the smile.

"And what about you?" the younger woman asked shyly.

"I," Nell told her, "am going to make good on the money I got from Deke. I am going to find a worthwhile—and legitimate—charity for terror victims' families and land the money on it. That's what the donations were intended for. And I'll see to it that two-thirds of the ghostwriting job funds end up there."

Patty stared at her.

"That's a lot of money. Can you afford to do that?"

Nell shrugged again.

"Can't afford not to, I guess. I am not a woman of great means, Patty, but I am comfortable, and I know that I have been blessed. Moreover, I believe that what goes around, comes around; therefore, other meaningful work is bound to come my way."

Nell finished her coffee. Or most of it. Then she stood to leave. She extended her hand to Patty who took it and started to shake it. But then Patty—the former Miss Dry Ice—pulled Nell toward her in an embrace. The two women stood for a while—quite a while—holding each other close.

"Oh," said Nell, as they gently separated, "I almost forgot!"

She stooped and reached into her quilted bag and drew out a quart jar of soup.

"It's chicken with rice," she explained, holding it out to Patty. "Chicken soup is beneficial. It helps heal."

∽

www.ingramcontent.com/pod-product-compliance
Lightning Source LLC
Chambersburg PA
CBHW020842260626
47169CB00003B/1104